WOE 1

WOE 1

2038–2048

A NOVEL

NATHAN SCOTT

This book is dedicated to God, our Heavenly Father. You have, over the span of my life, prepared me to deliver Your messages to the world, which concerns the relationship You desire to have with each of us and the relationship You desire for us to have with one another: relationships of love, care, and respect.

It is also dedicated to each reader who will receive and act upon the messages sent by God through His messengers.

CHAPTER
ONE

Good Friday, April 3, 2048—10:45 a.m.
Seattle, Washington

Mike and Rina were on their way to Seattle, Washington, in his father's private jet. They were approaching Mount Saint Helens.

The jet started its descent while banking around the top of the volcano, and a huge, black, smoky-looking cloud rapidly rose from the volcano's opening. There was a loud fluttering noise, and immediately, the plane was peppered with what sounded like small stones. One of the engines sounded like a giant blender crushing ice and began to smoke.

The pilot checked his gauges to note the status of that engine. He then heard a solid impact to the windshield and quickly looked to see a creature that resembled a nine-inch grasshopper. It had two sets of wings that fluttered like a hummingbird. The creature had the face of a man and long hair, and it appeared to have a gold crown on its head. Its body was shaped like that of a horse with an iron breastplate, its tail resembled that of a scorpion, and it had two hopper legs. When it turned and looked into the cockpit, it displayed lionlike teeth and seemed to growl.

The pilot looked at the copilot and screamed, "What the hell is that?"

They both looked at the windshield again. It had disappeared.

The copilot looked like he was in shock. When he responded, he said, "I can't admit to what I saw. I just got this job. Besides, they'll test me and know I had a martini late last night."

John's Vision, A. D. 95–96 (Approximately 1,952 Years Earlier)
Island of Patmos

My name is John, and as I sat on the shores gazing at the serenity of the sea, I heard a thunder that was so loud I thought my ears would burst. The sky began to peel itself away like an orange losing its outer skin. I could see an enormous titan-like figure sitting on what resembled a throne, and he glowed with many different colors. The light that shone around him resembled the brilliance of a rainbow. There was thunder and lightning, yet I saw no rain. I began to wonder what might have been in those beans I had for dinner. I could hear voices as they debated whether the time was right for some great event to take place. I could see only the great figure who sat on the throne-like chair, but I heard many different voices.

Then I began to see some strange-looking beasts, which appeared to be the ones whose voices I heard, speaking with about twenty-four human-looking figures that appeared in the midst of the sky.

These four beasts had eyes in the front and the back. One looked like a lion, one like a young cow, one like a large eagle, and one had the face of a man, but all of them had three sets of wings.

And then it just vanished. The whole scene was gone. As fast as it had appeared, it disappeared.

I thought that was the most bizarre incident of my whole life, but I was badly mistaken because for about a week, I kept having these crazy experiences. Every day a different one but with the same figure sitting on that throne, opening a book that had seven sections. Each section had a seal keeping it closed with a looping string.

The first morning after the initial vision, I awakened about an hour before daybreak. Again, I saw the great titan-like figure sitting on the throne. But this time, he looked like a young lamb. He was holding the strange book. When the lamb unwound the string binding the first section of the book, I heard a voice say, "Come close. Let me show you some things."

As I lay on my bed, looking into the darkness of the room's ceiling, it became bright with movement. There was an angel-like being flying around and around the ceiling, very fast at first, and then it slowed down. It stood in the midst of the ceiling, and from underneath its right wing, it pulled out what appeared to be some sort of horn, a trumpet probably. It blew the horn with one loud blast, which lasted about ten seconds, and then the being disappeared into a black cloud.

When it vanished, hailstones like balls of fire fell from the cloud, and the cloud glowed red and dripped raindrops of blood. As the flaming balls and blood fell to the ground, I could see grass burning until it was gone, and great trees were burned to black sticks. My heart was troubled, and my mind was perplexed by the vision, because as far as I could see into the horizon, much of the crops and a third of the trees were burned, and all manner of green grass was destroyed—gone.

What can this mean? *I thought. I prayed to God, who created it all, for this not to become a reality. I screamed in anguish, followed by loud crying and moaning.*

On the night of the second day after, I had a terrible time going to sleep, but before I could, I saw that angel-like being again—or perhaps it was another. This one seemed different somehow, I'm sure.

Nevertheless, I saw it. When it blew its horn, a huge mountain appeared, burning like a great torch, spewing fire. It then fell into a large body of water, maybe the sea.

The water began to look like blood. The blood consumed about a third of the water's volume. All sorts of fish and creatures that were in the affected waters died. I saw ships and boats having trouble powering through the tainted water; they began rolling over to their sides and sinking, and some turned upside down. A third of them sank and were lost—destroyed. I wondered if anyone I knew was on any of those vessels—maybe me, even. I don't know. The vision was over.

On the third day, I saw another angelic being flying among the stars of the heavens, circling one star and then another, as though it were looking for a particular type or size of star. After passing a few stars, it stopped before one huge star and blew its horn, and the star began trembling and shaking violently, as though it were trying to break loose from the atmosphere's hold.

Suddenly, it fell with tremendous speed toward the Earth with a tail of fire, like a flaming arrow that had been shot down from the heavens. As it got closer to the Earth, it began to break up into several pieces; each piece plunged into a river right where the waters were made clean and suitable for drinking. I heard the angelic being shout with a loud voice, "Wormwood, kill them by the tens of thousands, kill men!" I began to pray to the God of my father for reason of fear and enlightenment, but to no response.

On the fourth day after, as I sat looking into the sea again, I saw in the distant sky a flying figure moving between the sun and the moon. Back and forth it flew, quickly back and forth, then stopped between them. It took a horn from beneath its wing, pointed it at the sun, and blew. Turning around, it pointed it at the moon and blew it again. As the being vanished, I saw a third of the sun had been smitten, so I looked toward the moon, and it too was smitten, affecting one-third of its mass. When I looked at the stars, one-third of those too were smitten. One-third of the sun, the moon, and the stars did not give forth their light for one-third of the day.

I heard another angelic being shout, "Woe! Woe! Woe! To the inhabiters of the Earth by reason of the other voices of the trumpet of the three angels, which are yet to sound!" Because there were more major disasters to come upon humanity.

I was sorely wounded in my soul and wearied, yet I received no rest from my calling, for on the fifth day after, I saw a fifth angelic being standing between Heaven and Earth. When it blew its horn, I saw a star fall from Heaven and hit the Earth. I heard a voice speak and say to the star, "Herein is the key that releases your king and his mighty army, for their battle is near at hand."

While the voice yet spoke, a great key on a chain was handed to the star, and the voice said, "Open the bottomless pit, and release the armies of Abaddon, as known to the Hebrews, and known to the Greeks as Apollyon, who is their king."

With a loud cry, the king of the locusts from hell was summoned. "Abaddon/Apollyon!" he cried.

After I heard this, I saw smoke rise from the pit, so thick that the sun was not visible for a while. I saw locusts by the hundreds of thousands, millions, ascend from the pit. Then the voice said, "For five months, do not eat the food of your nature, no grass or leaves or plants of any kind. Hurt men who are not sealed; don't kill them but hurt them with a sting of terror and pain for five months. Let their flesh and skin be your food and their blood your drink, but not unto death!"

As the locusts swarmed to their king to be instructed, the sound of their wings was like the sound of many chariots pulled by many horses to a battle. They had teeth like a lion, tails with stingers like a scorpion, bodies like horses with breastplates of iron, and the face of men, and on their heads, it was as though they wore a crown of gold, with hair like a woman! I was moved to terror!

It seemed like I had slept for many days, dreaming dreams that I couldn't explain, seeing things that were so unbelievable, and then it was over. No more dreams, no visions—nothing!

As suddenly as it had started, it stopped.

CHAPTER
TWO

Rina Adelstein
May of 2028

Amir Adelstein was a seventeen-year-old high school senior. He and his family lived in a small village a few miles outside of Tel Aviv, Israel. His father, Aryeh Adelstein, was a police officer in Tel Aviv and made a good living, and his mother, Shiran Adelstein, worked in a pharmacy. Amir also had a younger sister named Rina.

There had recently been an increase of civil and political unrest in the region; Aryeh and Shiran were aware of the possibility their son might be summoned by the military for service. They were capable of sending him out of the country for college, so they spoke to Amir one morning during breakfast concerning the matter, offering him a chance to go to America.

"Amir," said his father. "My son, it is time to discuss your preparation for the future. What would you rather do: stay here and serve in the military or go to America for college?"

"Father, what would you advise me to do? You work as a police officer. Isn't that a great job to have?"

"It is a good job, but if all this bombing, protesting, and unrest continues, I could be transferred to the military. I don't want that for you. I'd rather have you be the first in my father's house to have a college education. Besides, it's a lot less dangerous than military service."

"America is such a large place and so far away. How will I survive there alone?"

"We'll make sure that you are well cared for there. Many of our people have gone to America, and many have chosen to stay."

"I'll go for the education and come back home afterward to teach here—maybe at my same school."

"It will be a big challenge, but I believe that you are capable of handling it. Your mother and I will make all the arrangements for you, but you must promise that you will stay out of trouble and finish your education, no matter how long it takes. You'll be the first; make us proud."

"I will not fail you, Father, and I will not fail you, Mother."

"You must continue to live by your Christian values and faith in America. Many have given their lives and their homes to come here to this Christian village to pave the way for the likes of us. We must continue to show our appreciation by never turning away from our faith."

"I never will, Father, Mother!"

* * *

Amir graduated high school and went to America, promising his parents to be a good example for his little sister Rina, who was now twelve years old and a seventh grader in junior high school.

After he graduated from the University of Washington in Seattle with a degree in engineering, he got a job in Dallas, Texas, at a manufacturing plant as a machine shop method engineer. During his frequent visits to the machine shop, he developed a working relationship with a toolmaker by the name of Jay Bolden, whom he had met in college. Within a couple of years, they became very good friends, spending many weekends and holidays together. When Jay married his girlfriend, Lauren, Amir was his best man and later became godfather to the couple's two children.

Rina kept in contact with her brother over the years, often asking him to come home and visit. Finally, he did so in 2033, when she was a senior in high school and he was twenty-two, working on his master's degree.

"Dear brother," Rina said, "tell me about going to college in America. I think I would like to go to the same school."

"College was not as hard as I had expected, but it is quite demanding. You must be diligent and focused on what you want to accomplish."

"Speaking of which, Father and Mother told me you are an engineer for a big manufacturing company in the machine shop sector. I thought you wanted to be a teacher."

"Yes, I changed majors twice, and knowing you, little sister, you'll probably change majors at least once every year!"

"No, actually, I already know how I want to spend the rest of my life after college."

"How might that be? Have you discussed this with Mother and Father?"

"Mother says she'll be happy with whatever I choose to do as long as I uphold my Christian beliefs. Father's not so sure anymore; Christians are being arrested and killed in many of the cities around here lately."

"Not in America. Though there are many different religions there, people are free to believe and worship to their liking."

"Are you certain?"

"As certain as I am good-looking."

"Mother has said on many occasions that your handsome face will either get you married or into a lot of trouble someday. So are you thinking of marriage? Or trouble?"

"I came home to celebrate your upcoming graduation, thank you! Speaking of college, have you decided where you'll go and what you'll study?"

"Father and Mother have already started arrangements for me to go to the University of Washington! I became quite interested in science, and I made all As and Bs. I *know*—not *think*—I want to be a scientist and chemist."

"Sounds like quite the challenge, but I believe if you dedicate the time to study and research, you can do it."

* * *

Amir's father had made sure his son would have a better life than he had in their little village. And as political turmoil grew to be an everyday norm in the Middle East, Amir's parents realized that it was not going to be a good place for Rina to go to college either. They convinced her that America would be the best place for her. She agreed under the condition that she could go to the same school as her brother. They all agreed, and when she graduated high school, she enrolled at the University of Washington as a science major. She had even received a full academic scholarship as a foreign exchange student.

When she had settled in, she called Amir and gave him the good news.

"Brother, hello! How are you, and where are you now living?"

"Ah, hello, sister! I'm well, thank you! I live in a small community called Arlington Park, near the hospital where President John F. Kennedy was taken when he was assassinated. I met this young man, Jay, at college and now work with him. We became good friends, and I visited his home on many occasions. I decided I wanted to live in the same neighborhood as him because it reminded me of home, in a way."

"What way?"

"It's a small neighborhood set off by itself, with probably less than a hundred families, but lots of pretty, single, young women."

"You mean lots of trouble."

Amir laughed. "Only joking about the women. Anyways, I hope you enjoy school in Seattle and your major undertaking in science and chemistry."

"I love science so dearly! It will be my life because I can think of no other field I'd rather study."

"That's good to hear! I'm glad you called, but I have a lot to do, so I've got to get off the phone. If you speak with Father and Mother, tell them that I love them and I'll call them later."

"I'll relay your message, and we'll all pray you'll get married soon and stop chasing after women. It's not good, it's not healthy, and it's not Christian-like."

"You're right again and again and once more again. Goodbye now!"

They hung up.

* * *

Rina's love had always been science; therefore, when she showed much promise in her first year of college, 2034, the top science professor, Professor Clarence Dodds, took her on as his protégé. By the time she was a senior, she was one of the best students he had ever taught. Several times, he let her teach during discussions of difficult subjects. She had become most proficient in discovering ways to better understand the far-fetched and the unknown. Professor Dodds became intrigued in helping her dig deeper into her mind to unlock more brilliance that he believed was waiting to be released.

Michael T. Lathan Jr.

During the same decade, there was a young man who was raised in a very prominent area of Dallas Texas, called Highland Park. His name was Michael T. Lathan—just like his father, a well-known and highly respected minister in the Methodist church. Michael Jr., who preferred to be called Mike, was a very bright boy early in his life and later desired to follow in his father's footsteps, going to college at Southern Methodist University in Dallas and getting a degree in pastoral ministries.

His father, Rev. Dr. Michael T. Lathan, Sr., at the time Mike was in college, was one of the most respected pastors in the country and often traveled abroad. He was frequently called to the White House to advise presidents in spiritual matters and for committee meetings and related purposes. It could be said he had become a White House favorite, being very active in politics for a few administrations.

Mike, against the advice of his father, wanted to minor in science, not political science. He was fascinated by every aspect of science, especially the weather and its interconnections with agriculture. He was bright enough to pull it off.

When he was a freshman at Southern Methodist University, science began to take over as his major field of study, but pastoral ministries were still advised, even demanded, by his father, who hoped his son would someday take over his duties as a senior pastor.

When Mike was a sophomore, one of his theology professors began to show a lot of admiration for his ability to read into the Scriptures and see what was meant, not stated. An ability or gift that was straight from God Himself, one might say. Rev. Dr. Donald Mason was his name, and he told Mike that he would like to take him under his wing. One of the pieces of advice given to most serious Bible scholar hopefuls is to find a great minister they admired and emulate their every action. Mike was quite aware of this because his well-celebrated father had pounded it into his head for years. Rev. Dr. Lathan would never have expected it to be someone other than himself.

Mike eased into the role of protégé to Rev. Dr. Mason, who invited him to several meetings and even allowed him to take over some of his classes when Mike was an undergrad student and after he graduated in 2037. They stayed in contact afterward, and Rev. Dr. Mason often visited him at his church and at his job as director of a science and engineering research laboratory. Mike's heart and career had begun to follow the direction of scientific research, and he was often invited to speak at Southern Methodist University science fairs and other conventions around the country. He soon became known among a very high-ranking group of national scientists. Even the president of the United States, President Tyler Turnkey had heard of his brilliance in not only science but the religious world as well.

Often rebuked by the religious world and warned by the great minds of modern science, Mike spent a lot of research time on both the Bible and the broad world of science, because he believed, deep in his heart, there had to be some tie-ins between the two. He desperately wanted to prove the dots were there and only needed to be connected, leading to some dual purpose for the good of humanity.

CHAPTER
THREE

Good Friday, April 23, 2038
Dallas, TX
(Centuries after John the Revelator's Vision)

While the Bolden family in Dallas, Texas, was out in the backyard chilling with some barbeque and drinks—some soft drinks, some not so soft—they heard a loud noise rush across the sky.

"Some jet must have broken the sound barrier," Jay Bolden said.

"Fool, they don't do that anymore," Jay's brother, Torey, responded.

"Well, whatever it was, it almost burst my eardrums."

Jay's cousin Billy, looking up toward the sky, said, "I don't know what it could have been. It's not cloudy or raining, so it couldn't have been thunder."

Almost everyone began to give their opinion of what they thought it was.

Courtney, the environmentalist cousin, called out, "Yeah, I bet global warming had something to do with it!"

"Maybe it was the sun farting," Jay suggested.

This drew some loud laughs. Then there was their gloom-and-doom aunt, Beatrice, letting everyone know that God was showing the drinkers that He was displeased with them.

Andy, one of the wayward relatives, said, "Uncle Tim, please take your prophetess wife home before she condemns us all to hell, because that would ruin my weekend."

"Will someone please turn that blasting music down? I'm trying to see if I can hear it again!" Beatrice yelled.

"There she goes again, Tim," his brother, Maurice, said. "Girl, why are you trying to break up this gathering? It's not even seven o'clock yet!"

"Will someone please go to the store? We're about to run out of ice," Billy said.

At that very moment, it began to hail—lightly at first—for about five minutes.

"Check that. Don't go to the store. Just get some freezer bags from the pantry!" Maurice said.

They all laughed frantically. But the laughter turned to serious concern when everyone noticed the hail was smoking. Some took cover in the garage, which was open, and others ran to the house. But Torey and Maurice stayed in the yard.

Maurice picked up one of the hailstones and said, "Now this is some freaky crap!"

As he held it in his hand, it burst into a white-and-red flame and oozed a reddish slime that resembled blood, which burned his hand and left a quick-rising blister that smelled like burned flesh. He screamed in pain while frantically trying to throw it to the ground because it was stuck to his hand, sizzling. The reddish slime coated his hand like melted wax.

When he finally got rid of it, it hit the ground, coated in his blood. They noticed that the hail striking the ground now looked like frozen drops of blood that smoked and steamed with fire and heat. The grass and some trees burst into flames, and people were jumping into their cars and trucks to get home and check on their houses and families.

The strange thing was that no houses were damaged, but about thirty percent of people's yards and trees were burning. Jay and his family and friends who had stayed could hear sirens from police and fire trucks going from one property to another. Fire trucks that came on the scene were running out of water, and they didn't have enough personnel to meet the community's needs. It didn't matter, because no amount of water worked. The red, smoking hail continued to burn and destroy trees and yards and fields for hours.

And as suddenly as it started, it stopped. Jay and the others rushed to turn on the news and see how bad it was. They learned that it was not isolated but was happening everywhere—every community, every town, city, state, and country—simultaneously.

Some of the friends who were at the cookout got on their cell phones to check on their families. One of those friends was Amir Adelstein, who was from a small village outside the city of Tel Aviv, Israel.

"Hello, Mother, are you OK?"

"My son, we are all well."

"Are you watching any of the news?"

"Yes, it appears that this is occurring all over. I was beginning to worry about you there."

"It's quite severe here. Trees and plants have been ruined everywhere, but few people were injured. Mother, have you heard from Rina? I haven't been able to reach her. Our connection won't go through."

"I just got off the phone with her. She's fine, but she's concerned about what all this means."

"Mother, Rina's calling me now. I'll check back in with you later."

"Be safe, my son. Tell your sister to call me when she gets off the phone with you. She said she'd call me back earlier but hasn't yet."

"Yes, Mother, I will tell her. Goodbye."

"Hello, Amir, how've you been? Have you talked with Mother?" Rina asked.

"I just hung up with her. She's worried about you, and you haven't called her back. She's wondering why."

"I was about to check on them before you called."

"Call her and let her know you're OK. By the way, how's the weather there in Seattle?"

"It's as strange here as it is almost everywhere else, I suppose. Brother, what do you think is behind this phenomenon?"

"Why do you ask me? You're the future scientist. Seriously, though, I don't know that there is an answer!"

* * *

Rina rushed out from the science building with Professor Dodds. As they entered the parking lot, they saw the effects of the hailstorm and immediately began to discuss possible causes of this strange occurrence. They had waited inside for some forty-five minutes for the hailstorm to cease, watching in fear and wonderment as the flaming balls dropped from the sky.

"Professor Dodds, is there a believable explanation for such a bizarre incident?" Rina asked.

"I can't think of any scientific history that can give any direction as to not only why but how could this have happened," Professor Dodds replied.

"I was taught that for everything that happens, there is an explanation. But as for whether there is a scientific one, that is to be determined."

"I wish I knew where to start! Hail that burns trees, plants, and human flesh but not houses or their roofs. The answer is out there somewhere, though, and we must find it."

"Wherever the answer is, I believe it's much bigger and more important than what we're seeing and experiencing."

"I was raised as a Christian, but when my mother died when I was only twelve years old, I couldn't believe that the God my parents taught me about would take my mother if He loved me so much. But I remember one particular Bible story that mentioned hail that burned with fire. As I got older and took an interest in science in high school, I couldn't see how that could happen, knowing that water can smother fire. So, what is hail but frozen water?"

"But Professor, I've handled hot ice, which can burn and even blister flesh," Rina said.

"But did it have a flame, as we've seen with this hail? Did it glow like fire? I think not! There lies the mystery."

"Could this be the same as the hail in your Bible story?"

"That stands to be proven," Professor Dodds said.

"I look forward to discussing more possibilities in our next class."

"Yes, I'll see you then," he said as he headed for his car, a worried expression on his face.

* * *

Meanwhile, back in Dallas, Torey and the others were trying to get home to their families. The traffic on every street was crazy. Hail would land on their vehicles and just stick, with the flames burning about two inches high but not damaging any of the paint.

People were panicking, with some stopping and trying to douse the hail with water, which only caused the flames to rise and glow brighter. Accidents were happening all over the globe. People were trapped in cars that were aflame, yet the burning hail was not damaging the cars themselves. When people got out of their automobiles, they saw no damage to their own vehicles or anyone else's. Everywhere, people were standing around looking and scratching their heads in shock and amazement. The conversations were not about who was in the wrong in terms of fender benders but what was going wrong to cause all this mayhem.

* * *

After most of their guests had left, Jay had gone back into the house, turned on his monitor, and clicked to the news to see what was going on elsewhere. Reporters were covering the events surrounding the hail and how world leaders were reacting.

A QUIK News anchorwoman reported, "We're hearing reports coming out of Europe that they are checking satellite images to see if the American government has been conducting any types of experiments with climate that might have contributed to this strange, never-before-seen phenomenon."

Robert Chance, another QUIK correspondent, reported, "President Tyler Turnkey and the defense secretary have been receiving threats from other countries promising nuclear attacks on US bases around the globe if they prove any US involvement."

NBS News reported, "China has not commented, but they have deployed fighter jets to scan above cloud formations, looking for clues. They also sent up survey planes to the edges of airspace boundaries."

Most of the world leaders' first responses were to activate some sort of military presence as a precautionary measure, not wanting to be caught off guard by anyone.

CHAPTER
FOUR

Broadcasting on the National Weather Channel, the World International Weather Channel, and other news outlets, the US president, President Tyler Turnkey, addressed the nation:

"We're asking all other world leaders to remain calm while we try our best to find out what is going on. We're working with our science departments and our top scientists from all our major institutions, and we promise the people of our great nation that we will get to the bottom of this. So, I'm asking everyone to please try to stay calm and exercise caution. It would be better not to go out unless it's totally necessary. I'll make another address when we have something definite to share."

* * *

President Turnkey called Dr. Boeddeker Bookman of the Office of Science and Technology Policy in Washington, DC, to put together a committee of professors from top science and meteorology universities from around the country, along with the director of the National Severe Storms Laboratory in Norman, Oklahoma. Their task was to deliver some sort of believable scientific reasoning for the burning balls of ice covered with a waxy, bloody substance, an oxymoron in its own right.

Professor Dodds received a phone call from a friend and former colleague. "Hello, Clarence, this is Boeddeker Bookman."

"Good afternoon, Doc. How's life treating you these days?"

"Well, despite the many reasons why I could, I won't complain. I'm calling because I've been tasked by the president to establish a committee to look into this worldwide event of this strange hail we've been experiencing. I need someone to head up this committee who can maybe get to the bottom of what's happening. Would you at least consider being my guy?"

"Yes, of course. If I may, I have a very bright exchange student I'd love to include. She has a knack for such challenges."

"Certainly, bring her along. I'll be busy putting together the rest of the committee for the next couple of days. When I'm done, I'll email you the information for the day, time, and place for our first meeting. By the way, what's your protégé's name?"

"Rina Adelstein. She's from Tel Aviv, Israel, and she's the senior class president."

"Sounds great. I look forward to meeting her. You'll hear from me again soon. Take care. Live well, my friend."

"You take care as well. See you soon, friend. Goodbye."

Professor Dodds called Rina.

"Hello, this is Rina."

"Hello, it's Professor Dodds. I just got off the phone with a very good friend and colleague of mine who works for the US Office of Science and Technology Policy at the White House. He's putting together a committee of scientists, meteorologists, and others to try to get some idea of what may have caused the strange and historical storms with the burning, icy balls of blood."

"Professor, you said 'strange,' and I relate to that description, but you also said 'historical.' Can you give me clarity on that account? I don't recall ever hearing of something like this before. Never!"

"Rina, you are a Christian, correct?"

"For certain I am. However, to practice it in the region where I was raised was and still is a dangerous thing."

"Well, there's a story describing how a similar hailstorm happened to the Egyptians by God's hand in the second book of the Bible, and it was prophesied to happen again toward the end of time in the last book."

"Does someone think there may be a connection?"

"That might be discussed, along with scientific matters. I don't know yet. Would you be interested in accompanying me to that meeting?"

"Wow! That would be grand. I'd love to go! Yes! Yes!"

"I'll contact you with the details later today."

"I'm so excited. I can't wait!"

"Look for a call from me in a few hours, OK?"

"Yes, sir, and thanks again! Goodbye."

Later that evening, Professor Dodds called Rina again. "Hello there. Can you make a late flight on Sunday the twenty-fifth?"

"Yes, you can pick me up at my dorm. Call when you're on the way so that I can be ready."

"Will do. I'll set up a couple of hotel rooms. See you then."

"Great!"

The hailstorm had stopped leaving behind the destruction of much of the world's trees, grass, and food crops.

Monday, April 26, 2038

The committee met for its first meeting, with all possibilities to be considered. Professors from the top science and meteorology universities and the director from the National Severe Storms Laboratory were there, and President Turnkey was in attendance.

During the brainstorming phase, an important question was brought up.

Professor Knobbs from the University of Oklahoma asked, "Are we to assume that ice can burn—to the point that it can destroy human flesh but not melt before hitting the ground? I wonder if there is any other explanation besides it just being a freak wonder of nature."

"We can't go before the world and say there's not a reason or a cause, and it's up to this committee to find them both, so put your heads and your degrees together. I want a possibility, at the very least," President Turnkey commented.

"Does anyone have a starting point?" asked Professor Dodds.

"Would a good starting point be that we don't have a clue about what in God's name is going on?" Professor Billingsley of Stanford University commented.

Director Diggs of the National Severe Storms Laboratory stated, "That might be the only starting point that makes sense."

"This is not some 1500 BC Bible riddle, sir," Professor Dodds said.

"Gentlemen," President Turnkey said. "Please, let's not take any possibilities off the table. Rather, let's list as many as we have and seriously work with one another until the best one becomes the most likely one. Let's start by recording this one and global warming as another. If we must meet every day or for however long it takes, we desperately need a viable pool of reasons and possibilities. Let's get serious. The public needs our expertise to produce something that makes them feel safer. I will contact some of our leading clergies and spiritual advisors."

The committee, along with the president, brainstormed for the next two hours, and the committee continued to meet for the next three days.

CHAPTER
FIVE

Tuesday, April 27, 2038

Earlier that day, President Tyler Turnkey, had set up a late-evening meeting via holographic telepresence with his spiritual advisors and some of the country's most prominent clergies: Father Nathan Matthews, a Catholic Cardinal; Dr. Lucas Timothy, an Evangelical; Bishop Mark Soloman, a Pentecostal; Rev. John Coverton, a Baptist; Dr. Cynthia Scott, an Independent Nondenominational; and Rev. Dr. Donald Mason, a Methodist along with his protégé, SMU theology graduate Michael T. Lathan Jr.

During the meeting, questions were asked concerning the possibility of biblical ties to the current event. President Turnkey asked, "Does anyone here have reason to believe that there may be something more here than just a cosmic phenomenon that inadvertently occurred? Or is there some message that the higher power we know as God may be trying to get us to see?"

"With all due respect, Mr. President," Dr. Lucas Timothy responded. "Our government has gotten to the point of passing laws that are directionally opposite to the teachings of our Holy Bible.

God's not at all happy about it. We must understand that when any governing body removes God's principles from its decision-making process, especially when it affects the moral purity of His people, consequences are likely. In this case, let us ask ourselves, are there laws that punish God's people for standing up for His Word? If we can see reasons for His judging our laws, there could be a connection."

"So are you saying that there is a connection? Can you produce evidence in Scripture where the Bible specifically addresses laws that *may* seem to be contrary to its teachings? We cannot present to the public mere speculation on how scientific events and Scripture collaborate to indict the government for its stand on majority and even minority beliefs. I have to see with my eyes—not my heart, not my moral beliefs—or my personal sense of understanding that some or all of our laws are leading this country as a whole to disobey the commandments of the Bible, and therefore fiery hail is the punishment, which destroyed food and vegetation, which I'm sure you would agree were given to the world by God—the God who declares in His Word that He loves us. Show me where it says that this food will be burned by the fire of burning ice!

"I'm sure that at least some of you say that is exactly the case, and it may be. But all I'm asking is for foolproof evidence of that claim. I need you to understand my position as the commander in chief who leads not only the people of this great nation but the people of the entire free world. All nations are depending on us for answers. You see, I can't afford speculation or philosophical voodoo. I want us to work together as a problem-solving team without conflict, with one common goal: to appease the confusion of the people. If there is something there in the Bible, believe me when I say that I truly and desperately want to see it and understand it. Show me where the Bible says that if God doesn't like our laws, He will send us burning hail as a sign of His anger and disapproval."

"All I ask is that you examine our governing laws and cross-reference the Bible. If you are a true believer, make your own decision, sir," Dr. Timothy replied.

President Turnkey moved on to Father Matthews, asking, "Father Matthews, what have you, if anything, considered on this matter?"

"Mr. President, we have mountains filled with smoldering lava all over the Earth. These constantly erupt—some even explode—costing millions of dollars in damage and resulting in tens of thousands losing homes and their lives. This has happened for millions of years, and no one can accurately say whether they are acts of God or just merely acts of nature. Our planet is an active volcano that may one day explode. Who can predict it? Who can explain the whys, wheres, whens, or ways? I wouldn't be so fast to say God caused this hail or to say it was for some gross disobedience. I do, in my heart, believe it was just nature reacting by its own nature."

"You know, Father Matthews, I believe that a great percentage of the people of this country and others would agree with that belief. Scientifically, it makes a lot of sense. Yet we would do well not to totally rule out any other possibilities for this occurrence. Keep in mind, everyone, that the event that we're discussing was not confined to our nation only but experienced by all nations around the globe, almost simultaneously, with exactly the same degree of destruction, which would classify it as not only strange but almost planned. But again, I'm not yet endorsing either theory; rather, I'm looking for believable facts—or, shall I say, stronger evidence."

President Turnkey asked Dr. Cynthia Scott next, "Dr. Scott, what can you put on the table?"

"Sir, I've heard much conversation concerning the fiery hail that fell upon Egyptian soil, and God hardened Pharoah's heart to not allowing God's people to leave at that time. Considering that it was not immediately effective in forcing Pharaoh's decision to free his people, I'm not certain that God would choose to use it again. But in the New Testament, John stated that he saw it happening toward the end-time, but when it would happen, John didn't say. It would be difficult to say that right now the end of days is upon us. Too many other things need to happen. So, Mr. President, there is the possibility that God is involved, but there's also the possibility He's not. I think, though, the answer could be some cosmic debris coming into contact with our atmosphere and, though frozen, catching fire before coming in contact with the Earth."

"Dr. Scott, I'm certain that one mistake we surely don't want to make is to predict the end of time as we know it here on Earth. Far too many have made that mistake in the past, and some are still making it today, but we won't join that coalition! Many would say that what happened to Pharaoh was in the almost forgotten past and that what John wrote that he saw will happen in the distant future, centuries after we're all dead and gone. Yet others will argue that we're living in the last days. But when is the end-time? I've heard it said, like all of you, that we're living in those days now. I believe we're moving toward those days, not living in them. That's the one thing that's absolute: those days are coming for each of us. Mine might be tonight, but I hope not. Who can say when their time ends? But it *is* coming.

"Bishop Soloman, what do you determine to be an explainable reason, and what do you think concerning the possibility of the end-time in our lives?" President Turnkey asked.

"With all due respect to yourself and the clergy present, we are indeed servants of the Most High God. Yet I've heard more political correctness today than in the last two presidential elections combined. God's Word is and always has been the Law of not only His people but for all people, and those of us who choose not to recognize it or not to profess it will not change that one fact. It stands to reason that all people are affected because all of us have loved ones who are believers and nonbelievers as well. Political correct-ness is OK if we're only trying to get votes, but I'm after neither votes nor popularity. The Word is what it is—not only spiritual teachings and advice but warnings as well. Ignoring the warning part of the Word does not change the penalty for such ignorance, and it may even hasten the inevitable.

"What has happened has happened, but I'm sure that this was just a preview of what is about to take place. Righteousness won't change the future events but for the righteous. Sir, there is nothing anyone can do to help everyone. But everyone can help themselves by adhering to God's warnings. So as far as this hail we just had, try to put it behind us and go forward spiritually in righteousness, both naturally and politically!"

"Bishop Soloman, I deeply appreciate the candidness and your deep-rooted belief and faith," President Turnkey responded. "May I assure you that I'm not after political correctness! However, we, as a team committed to resolving the mystery surrounding these recent happenings, must stay open-minded and respectful of one another's faith and beliefs.

"Yet I'm aware that some indifference exists concerning different denominations. But I chose each of you because I believe you to be among the elite of your individual groups, and I'm sure we can and will reach a conclusion we're all comfortable with. Because of the worldwide magnitude of what's happening now, we can't afford to put it behind us just yet, as much as I'd like to. We've got lots of work to sort out. I understand that although it sounds insensitive, gloom and doom may even seem to be the law of recompense. I believe there to be a more subtle explanation without totally discarding the spiritual laws and penalties. So, let's work in the known now. I just want to get a feel for where we may be headed."

"I think it is most important not to remove any thoughts or ideas from the table until we can agree on the spiritual, the natural, and the sensible," Bishop Soloman replied.

"Well said, Bishop, and I agree with that," President Turnkey said. "How about you, Rev. Coverton? What strikes you as a reason behind these events all over the world?"

"With all due respect to you, sir," Rev. Coverton responded. "I'd rather piggyback on the bishop's thoughts, if I may. Indeed, he spoke well, yet much can be said to confirm the thoughts of all who have spoken thus far. I am, however, of the mind that no matter which way we go forth from here, with much prayer and fasting, we can control our future outcome."

"Thank you as well. Rev. Dr. Mason, pleased as always to see you again. Good to see Mr. Lathan with you. A fine young minister he's grown to become. Share with us, if you will, and allow your protégé that opportunity as well," President Turnkey said.

"All respect to you, Mr. President. It's my pleasure to be a part of such a celebrated group of clergymen. First, let me introduce my good friend and understudy—who, by the way, Mr. President, has received his graduate degree in the field of science to complement his master's degree in theology. This is Mr. Michael T. Lathan Jr.

"Now, I've heard much testimony from different points of understanding, mostly in relation to God's position with respect to the present events around the globe. I can say that I agree with all that has been voiced because there are many variables that might suggest God's involvement. And I disagree as well because much of the evidence can suggest a good case for a scientific explanation.

"Now, before anyone accuses me of double-talk or straddling the fence, let me suggest that there's plenty of room to prove both if we stay completely open-minded. And before we, as clergy of the Most High God, declare that we're the only entity that can possibly explain what's going on, let's open the door of opinion and fact to other organizations in an open joint meeting and put every possibility on the table, whether spiritual, natural, or scientific.

"This brings me to the point of why I invited Mr. Lathan here today. I'm sure he'll have very valuable input on this matter in forthcoming meetings. So, without further delay, I present to you Michael Lathan Jr., or Mike, as he prefers to be addressed."

"President Turnkey," Mike said. "It's such a privilege to be in your honorable presence. Good morning, madam and gentlemen, to you all. I believe very strongly in defending the comments of Rev. Dr. Mason, whom I have so much faith in and respect for. His idea of a joint meeting with clergy and science could produce much, not only understanding but solutions as well. But as he stated, all of us must stay open-minded and respectful of one another's thoughts and beliefs. I'm certain that much can be accomplished. I don't know about you, but personally, I not only look forward to the challenge but embrace it."

Mike then relinquished the floor, and the president wrapped up the meeting, stating, "I'd like to review all that's been voiced, and my office will be contacting you soon. I thank you all for your time and your input. The meeting is adjourned."

Outside the meeting, in almost every crowd, there was someone pronouncing the end of the world or the harsh punishment of God. Ministries from every denomination and the nondenominational alike were seizing the opportunity right off the bat to hit the streets and airways, sharing their thoughts and beliefs.

CHAPTER
SIX

All the major news stations were covering this most strange event. Some were saying maybe former Vice President Al Gore was right in his claim of global warming, and some were blaming it on a second ice age starting, but none had a clue as to what the truth was. The emergency rooms were packed with the brave of heart but burned of hand—unsuspecting men, women, and some young children not seeing the danger of their curiosity.

World leaders were baffled as they chatted with one another from nation to nation. People everywhere were calling to check on their loved ones. Everyone was in awe that no homes were damaged. However, it was discovered that many food crops had been destroyed. Many trees—some that were hundreds and even thousands of years old—had been destroyed in just a few hours.

As the news spread about the lost crops, the stock market began to react. Farmers all around the world were told that they would receive less for their crops in an attempt to prevent price gouging at the markets. One particular potato farmer in Idaho met with a representative of the US Department of Agriculture at the local office.

"I'm sorry, Mr. Cartwright," the agriculture representative said.

But there's nothing I can do to change this pricing that's been imposed. This comes from the national level and is consistent for all farmers, no matter the crop. All pricing has been dropped by the same ratio according to demand in the marketplace for each crop."

"Man, I'm all for doing what's good for our citizens, even our exports, but it's going to be tough for me to seed another crop at this cost. In two seasons, I'll be bankrupt," Mr. Cartwright replied.

"Mr. Cartwright, I can assure you we won't let that happen. We know it's not what you're expecting to be paid, maybe not what you deserve, but to make the best of a bad situation, we'll all have to make some sacrifices. You can be assured that it's going to be a joint effort from us all."

Later that day, a meeting was called with the secretary of agriculture and the president to discuss the stock market backlash that was certain to occur.

"I know that some price gouging will take place, but is there anything that can be done to minimize the effects?" President Turnkey asked.

"There are no certain predictions at this moment, Mr. President, but let's see how the market opens and closes."

"We can't allow food costs to get out of reach for our citizens! Don't do what you can. Do what's necessary! Do what's right!"

"Sir, with all due respect, there's no way to predict the world market and how imports will be affected," the agricultural secretary replied.

"Do what's necessary! Do what's right! This meeting is over. I have a lot to consider and do. Please try to have a good weekend."

* * *

A few days later, President Turnkey had a staff member set up a holographic telepresence meeting with the NASA research team located at Johns Hopkins University. He started the meeting.

"Good morning, team," he said. "I am sure you are all aware of the phenomenon that took place ten days ago. We here at the White House and Pentagon are exhausting all possible measures to find some believable cause or explanation for this occurrence. The reason I contacted you is to see if you noticed any unexplained activity above our atmosphere that may have been detected by any of our long- or short-range satellites."

Dr. Thomas Kernny, director of the NASA research team, stated, "Mr. President, we've been actively looking into these happenings—not only here in the homeland, but we've also been contacting research teams in Russia, China, Germany, Canada, and several other countries and receiving similar reports. There's nothing outside what we've come to expect: exploding planets that have been in existence for millions—even billions—of years, the constant expansion of the universe, and stars appearing and disappearing."

"You know, Dr. Kernny, it is indeed the same story even at the Defense Department and National Security Agency. Nothing has been detected with our ground telescopes and short- to medium-range satellites. It's as though this hail appeared out of nowhere inside our own atmosphere all around the globe simultaneously. Another strange thing about it is that everywhere, the damage is the same ratio: one out of every three trees destroyed, one-third of every field, orchard, and grove destroyed. The consistency in the destruction ratio in itself is a phenomenon, and again, the most powerful minds in the world are left almost totally blank. Where do we go from here?"

They continued this discussion for some time yet couldn't reach any firm conclusions. The president closed by saying, "Well, let's continue our research and efforts to find answers, and we will meet at a later date."

* * *

Meanwhile, back at the Boldens, Tim Bolden's wife, Beatrice, shopped at the meat market. She called out to the on-duty butcher, "Hey, I was just in here the other day, and I think all your meat prices have gone up by around forty-four cents per pound. In just a couple of days? Come on, how can that have happened?"

"Yes, ma'am, I can show you on my delivery invoice the cost difference from the last shipment. It has to do with how the price for grain and hay and other animal feed has gone up for farmers and stockyards as well."

"Well, I want to see it! I ain't kidding either!"

"Sure thing. Andrew, hand me that invoice from my office. It's on the right side of the desk in the incoming tray."

Andrew went to the butcher's office and got the invoice. "Here it is," Andrew replied, handing it to the butcher, who then gave it to Beatrice.

Beatrice examined it and said, "I tell you, it's getting harder to feed a family day by day. Well, I hope this doesn't last too long."

On her way home, Beatrice saw a couple of men in suits carrying signs about two blocks from the market. On one side, the signs read, THE DAY OF RECKONING IS COMING TO THE WORLD, and on the other side, they read, THE END IS AT HAND! As she stopped at the corner, she could hear them preaching with Bibles in hand.

One man with a sign said, "Hello, miss, are you saved? Have you received God's mark in your heart?"

"Don't you mean on my forehead?"

"It doesn't matter if you have it on your forehead or the back of your head, as long as you have it."

The other man said, "Come on, man, stay saved."

"Well, it's apparent that she doesn't have it anywhere."

"Can you be so sure?" Beatrice asked. "Are you willing to wager your own salvation on it? Apparently, you may not be totally sold out yourself. You should check that attitude in at the nearest altar!"

One of the men said, "My sister, you have a blessed day. Stay righteous and be prepared for the end of time as we know it."

Upon arriving home, Beatrice couldn't wait to tell Tim of the spike in food prices and her encounter with the corner preachers. She hollered out, "Honey, do you remember the commercial with the cows telling people to eat more chicken?"

"Yeah, baby, that was a funny one. Been a while since I saw it, though."

"Well, I'm inclined to take the cows' advice, because even though the price of all meats is higher, beef is through the roof, and so soon after the hail destroyed so much vegetation."

"They've been talking about it on the news. It's getting crazy! Hope it turns around before long. I was talking to Billy and Courtney this morning. They were telling me how the hail caused accidents on their way home. Both of their cars were damaged. The streets were a mess, according to news reports."

As they began to channel surf, the situation was the same: total confusion everywhere with everyone. Of course, many clergies were bringing up the hail of Egypt in the days of Moses. Though it also had been mixed with fire, there had been no blood in it.

Hundreds of people were being questioned by the media all over the world. Tens of thousands of stories were noted. There were people whose hands were burned, and some had burns all over their bodies—serious burns. Most of these wounds were resistant to all ointments, rubs, and medications. Nothing healed them, and nothing eased their pain. People were seeing burn specialists, yet the nature of the burns was so bizarre that even the specialists were at odds as to the nature of the wounds and the best course of treatment.

Tim mentioned to Beatrice, "One person at a local hospital jokingly stated that this gives a new meaning to hot ice, noting that there is nothing amusing about the suffering of so many people. One of my nephews is a die-hard thrill seeker who never passes up a dare, and he refused to get within three feet of any of those hailstones. I heard one woman say that she'd been burned at least a hundred times —cooking, ironing, and pressing hair—but has never experienced anything that hurt so badly.

"One teen who had been burned and taken to the emergency room at that hospital was questioned as to why she thought this might have happened to her. As she cried in pain, she apologized to her mother for disrespecting her the day before because she believed she was being punished. Her friend scolded her and asked, 'What about all these others? Are they being punished?' She cried and answered, 'Must be for something.'"

* * *

By 2039, a year later, people were still trying to resume their lives and deal with the aftereffects. Strangely, many of the signs of the wounds, though they were burns, began to disappear, leaving no trace of injury. But the pain was a constant reminder of that horrific day.

CHAPTER
SEVEN

Good Friday, March 30, 2040

Two years had passed since the hailstorm of burning, bloody balls of fire. People were still talking about that event, of course, and the pain was a constant reminder to those who had been injured, but they had grown somewhat accustomed to it and didn't notice it as much anymore.

The Good Friday holiday is being observed in certain parts of the world when, simultaneously, two loud booms were heard on naval vessels at sea, one in the middle of the Atlantic Ocean and the other on the Pacific Ocean. Both were hundreds of miles from the coast, and the sounds were not clearly heard by anyone on land.

First Mate Miguel Mendez, who was on the Atlantic Ocean naval vessel, turned to a sailor he was having lunch with and asked, "What the hell was that?"

"I didn't hear anything, guy. You've been out here too dang long," the sailor replied.

"Yeah, I have, but it sounded like a jet, only much louder."

"You're just thinking too loud, that's all."

Meanwhile, those on the Pacific vessel heard a similar sound, but it was more like an explosion, which sent sailors running to their battle stations. The radar operator was frantically trying to pick up any signal he could at sea or in the air, but there was nothing. Then, with the aid of a pair of binoculars, First Mate Tom Powell spotted movement in the sky: a mountain-size flaming rock was hurtling toward the ocean at the speed of a jet flying at Mach 2.

He could see enormous waves being pushed up from the mountain splashing into the sea.

On the Atlantic side, a mountain of the same size did exactly the same thing: it plunged into the water, but in this case, everything around it was sucked to the ocean's bottom.

* * *

The vessel on the Pacific had been at sea for fourteen months, and everyone on board had been anticipating shore leave. They were only two days from furlough. Now, two hours after the mountain had plunged to the bottom, some of the sailors were on deck to see if they could spot land. They knew that they were near the Marshall Islands and were anxious to see the shore. Someone noticed a large school of fish they were approaching, but the fish seemed to be floating instead of swimming.

When the ship was almost on top of the fish, someone yelled out, "These fish are dead, all of them—hundreds, thousands. All kinds of sea life, all dead! People! I see dead people and pieces of boats and ships!"

"What could have caused this?" a sailor asked.

"You know, a couple of hours ago, I thought I saw something. I thought it was a mirage at first," First Mate Powell commented.

"A mirage is seeing water in the desert where there is no water, you fool. Not seeing water where there is water!"

"No, no, man, really. I thought I saw a mountain fall from the sky very, very fast and go into the water!"

"A mountain? Really! How the heck did you make first mate?"

"I'm serious, guy. I know what I saw."

"Well, what happened to the tidal wave? It should have washed us to land at seven hundred fifty miles per hour or to the bottom of this ocean even faster."

Looking at the captain, the first mate said, "I can't explain it, Captain, but I saw it. I don't know what it could mean, but I know I saw it."

Captain Brown said, "Go to the sick bay. I'll check on you later!"

By the time the captain got to the bridge, distress signals were coming up on the monitoring screens by the tens.

"What's happening, sir?" a sailor asked.

"Don't know yet, son," Captain Brown replied, "but I'm going to get to the bottom of it. You bet I will! Communications, contact Control and see if they know what's going on. Let them know we're in secure mode."

The USS *Fight*'s communication officer followed his order. "Control, come in, Control. Do you read me?"

"Loud and clear, sir. What's going on out there? We're getting strange activity on our tracking radar."

"Sir, where do I start?"

"Well, how about with the strangest event?"

"First Mate Powell noticed a very large object moving across the sky after hearing a loud booming sound. He watched as this object crashed into the ocean and disappeared while pushing up large waves. Hours later, we began to see debris from other vessels and all kinds of sea life dead, even corpses being carried by water currents toward this object. The captain has cleared us for recovery purposes."

"Just how large of an object was it, sir?"

"Reported to be as large as a mountain," the captain interjected.

"Be more specific. Just how big of a mountain did he see?" the control personnel asked.

"That's unclear. It was from miles away," Captain Brown replied.

"Do what you deem necessary while maintaining a safe distance. Keep us updated every four hours."

"Copy that and out. Gentlemen let's save what and who we can while keeping our eyes peeled for any signs of trouble. Communications, scan for sounds, especially distress signals. We've got a lot of work ahead. Tune your minds, people," the captain commanded.

Later that night, the communications officer called Control for the check-in. "Come in, Control, this is the communication officer aboard the USS *Fight*. We should be contacting the first crippled vessel by daybreak and the second by nightfall. Will contact Control then."

"We copy that."

"Calls are coming in from a radius of hundreds of miles! There are so many. How can we handle all of them?"

"Try to notify other ships that may be in the grid."

"We'll get as many as we can for as long as we can. Over and out."

"Copy that. Out."

"Sir," First Mate Powell said to the captain. What's going on with all these disabled vessels? From what I'm getting, some reddish, thick, sticky substance is contaminating their fuel and oil. It's choking out their engine power and causing severe knocking of blades in the turbines. Might be causing some bad foreign object damage."

"Let's head to the engine room. Notify our lab team to prepare for some FOD testing of the liquid type."

"Yes, sir. I hope we make it. Our blades are dicing a lot of fish, and that's gumming up the works."

Captain Brown entered the engine room and ordered, "Pulsate

the turbines to shake that gunk off, and give me a power output report by twenty-two hundred hours."

"Yes, sir," an engine room tech replied.

As morning approached, there was a horrible stench in the air from the dead sea life and corpses on the hot sea. As day began to break, the first vessel was in sight. There was a rusty-colored gloom above the seawater, but it was hard to make out what it was. A lab tech was summoned to take samples and test them.

About an hour and a half later, Dr. Collin Justin, the lab tech, entered the captain's quarters and asked, "Sir, can rocks bleed?"

"Speak with clarity, Doctor."

"Sir, this is blood, and a third of its makeup is rock dust," Dr. Justin said.

"You spent twelve years in medical school to come up here and tell me that a rock is bleeding into the Pacific and a third of its makeup is stone? Is this what you're telling me? Doctor, do you need some time on land as well? Am I to believe that these vessels may have stone-blood damage? What the hell kind of FOD is that? Is that what you want me to tell my commander? What about my career? No way! Go back to the lab, take another sample without rocks in it, and bring me an answer I can believe. Got it?"

"Yes, sir!"

* * *

In the meantime, the ship on the Atlantic, the USS *Washington-Goldwater*, was being pulled in the direction of the splashdown of the other smoldering mountain. The crew members were receiving hundreds of distress calls as well as signals from smaller boats that were being similarly drawn to the area of the splashdown much faster than the vessels could move under their own power. The smaller ones were being pulled into a moving sinkhole ten times the size of Niagara Falls. Ships by the hundreds were being destroyed, and sailors by the thousands were being dragged to a watery grave at the bottom of the Atlantic Ocean.

Being one of the US Navy's most powerful vessels, the warship was able to maneuver away from the sinkhole and convey the incident to the Pentagon. Speculations were raised regarding whether the Russians or the Chinese were responsible. Ten nuclear submarines from five different countries were deployed to investigate the happenings—five to the Atlantic and five to the Pacific.

The first sub to reach the Atlantic site began to experience severe turbulence in the form of underwater currents that spun around and around. The crew detected metal objects that were caught in the currents, thousands of them, both large and small. They were astounded to make out ships, boats, barges, and even oil rigs being sucked in and thrown out of the current's pull. Bodies were everywhere—fish, people—as well as uprooted sea plants and dislodged and broken reefs. It was a scene from a horrible disaster movie. The only thing they could do was make sure they didn't join the other vessels already caught in the current's pull.

The commander of the USS *Washington-Goldwater*, Captain Walter Wright, was in survival mode and barked out orders one after another. "Reverse engines! Engine room, give me all you got!"

An engine room tech yelled out, "Captain Wright, sir, we're almost at max reverse!"

"I don't want almost max. Get me max!"

They could see the sinkhole from a mile away, and they were getting closer. Captain Wright yelled, "I will not lose this vessel or my crew! Get us to max reverse!"

After a while, they broke free of the strong pull and started a sweep of a mile and a half in radius so that they could get a 360-degree view of this phenomenon. The maneuver proved to be as dangerous as the pull current itself. They were almost hit by several objects caught in the force of the current, vessels large and small that were not able to break free.

Suddenly, a loud bang resounded as a part of an oil rig platform slammed into the port side of the ship, almost top-siding it. Several of the crew were injured, and some were thrown overboard, but most were in the ship's cabin area. Captain Wright was tossed into the side of the windowed wall of the control room and knocked unconscious. First Mate Mendez assumed command and ordered a wider arc to look for any possible rescues.

The news of these two terrible events was broadcast all over the world. Ships, boats, rigs, and platforms from many nations were in both oceans. Scientists and academics from all countries were being called in. Air force, navy, and coast guard forces from around the globe were pitching in their efforts to help one another, and the world leaders held an emergency summit meeting.

As if matters weren't bad enough, debris was washing up along all shorelines at incredible speeds—vessels, bodies, crumpled metal, and rotten fish. Much of it was entangled in strange-smelling seaweed, which people were instructed not to touch. But in their efforts to help, people were frantically trying to clean the beaches and shores. This went on for months. The phenomena of the tidal pull in the two oceans continued as if they were motor-driven, constantly pulling and turning. The world's governments ordered all ships docked.

The captain of one of the nuclear subs was determined to get close to the gigantic "Atlantic rock," as they called it, now sitting on the bottom of a ten-mile-deep section of the ocean, but the sub began to experience enormous pressure around its hull and had to withdraw. It was ordered to stay close on guard for any new developments.

CHAPTER
EIGHT

Good Friday, April 19, 2041

On this night, several people from various countries saw objects shoot from the sky and thought they might have been meteors. They were so bright that they lit up the entire sky. The meteors fell upon one-third of the Earth's rivers and springs, which became polluted with wormwood.

The Following Days

Beach bum Jack Vanderful, not realizing the dangers around him, walked the beach night and day, noting everything that washed ashore at this Canary Islands, North Africa, location. He walked in the seaweed that washed ashore for days until his feet began to turn green. By the time he noticed them, he had begun to act strangely, paranoid about seeing human skeletons and monsters walking on six legs up and down the beach, seeking people to eat. Dead and live ones alike were being consumed.

Jack's brother was concerned and tried to talk to him. "Jack, who were you screaming at on the beach?"

"Come on, Don, I know you saw them—the beasts with six legs —eating those poor dead people."

"I think you should see a doctor."

"I'll go, Don, but there's nothing wrong with me."

Upon arriving at Dr. Murray Murphy's office the next day, when they walked into the examination room, Jack saw a skeleton model hanging on a rack and asked, "Doc, was he on the beach yesterday?"

Dr. Murphy looked at him in disbelief. "Sit on this stool, Jack. I want to examine you."

"I feel great, Doc, never better."

"Doctor, look at his feet," Don interjected. "What do you think could have caused that? They're a strange green—dark, dark green."

After looking at them closely, the doctor said, "Whoa! Jack, I'd like to do some blood work if it's OK with you."

"Sure, Doc, get on with it."

After drawing blood from Jack, a nurse sent it to the lab. Dr. Murphy said, "Come back in a couple of days, and we'll discuss my findings."

A few days later, before leaving Jack's home, Don called to make sure the doctor was ready for them to return.

"Yes, come in as soon as you can," Dr. Murphy said.

When they got there, the doctor greeted them with a befuddled look on his face. He said, "Jack, come into my office. We need to talk."

"OK, Doc, but I want Don to come in with me." Noticing the skeleton again, Jack said, "I know I saw him on the beach the other day being eaten by that ugly beast."

"OK, that's it!" Don exclaimed. "Doctor, what's going on with him?"

"He has a form of some hallucinatory drug in his system."

"Darn it, Jack, you fell off the wagon!"

"Hold on, Don. This is something I've never seen before—something very potent and very dangerous. It's eating away at his brain cells like a cancer, only at a much faster rate. How long has he been like this?"

"He was fine a few days ago when we had lunch together."

"I need him in the hospital for observation."

* * *

Meanwhile, tragic stories were pouring in from all over the world. At Daytona Beach, Florida, a famous surfer, Warren Weaver, began acting strangely. While hanging around the beach waiting for a challenging wave, Todd, who was with him, saw a distant look on Warren's face as he dropped his surfboard and started walking into the ocean.

"Where you going, fella? You forgot your board! Besides, I don't see any waves worth trying. Warren! What are you doing, man?" Todd asked.

"Don't worry. I'm just going to get a beer."

"A what? Out there? Are you OK?"

"Just watch my board. I'll be right back." He began laughing uncontrollably.

"You're freaking me out, man! I'm serious. You've gone far enough!"

By then, the water was up to Warren's neck, and he seemed not to be fazed or afraid. Todd dropped his board and ran toward Warren, but before he could reach him, Warren vanished and was swept away by a riptide.

"Lifeguard! Lifeguard! My friend just disappeared and didn't come back up!" Todd yelled.

Two lifeguards heard his calls and went into action, one carrying a floatation device and the other wearing flippers. After about seven minutes of searching for Warren, they both returned.

"Tell us what happened," the taller lifeguard said.

"Warren, my friend, started acting strangely and saying he was going to get a beer. I thought he was joking until the water passed his shoulders. Then I knew something wasn't right. I called for him to return, but he kept walking and laughing, so I ran toward him, and then he went under. I dove down but could not see him, and I knew he was in big trouble when I felt an underwater current moving outward. I came to the surface and made it back to the shallows, then called for you guys."

"I know Warren well. We were lifeguards together in junior high and high school. And I know he's a strong swimmer. I don't get it!" the shorter lifeguard said.

"I know he doesn't do drugs; he's been clean for years. Heck, man, he doesn't even drink. That's why I thought he was kidding around when he said he was going to get a beer," Todd responded.

The beach police arrived, and after hearing the details from Todd and the lifeguards, they called for a rescue squad, which searched until dusk.

"Man, I hate to be the one to tell his mom. He was an only child. But it has to be done," Todd said.

"Well, we can take care of it. Just give us her name and number," one of the beach police said.

"That's OK. I'll do it. She'd want me to be the one," Todd replied.

"I understand. But this is the scene of an accident. We'll have to contact the next of kin and interview her about his actions for the past few days."

When the beach police spoke with Warren's mother a few hours later at her home, the investigating officer asked her, "What has your son's attitude been like? Has he been depressed, angry, or acting strangely lately?"

"Not really, but yesterday morning, he complained of a slight headache and light-headedness."

"Did it seem to get worse as time passed?"

"Not that I could detect. I did notice some type of discoloration of his feet while he was walking around barefoot yesterday evening."

"What color were they?"

"A sort of light greenish, I suppose. It didn't look alarming. I just thought he was spending a little too much time in the water. Please! Have you found my son yet?" She began to cry.

"No, ma'am, not yet, but we've done all we can for the night. The search will continue at daybreak."

"I understand, sir. Thank you very much."

* * *

In the city of Oakland, California, Keith Renfro and his family were driving home after having dinner at a local seafood restaurant. Katherine, his wife, began shaking, then started screaming uncontrollably.

"Katherine, baby, what's wrong?" Keith cried, alarmed. "What's going on? Dang it, I knew we shouldn't have gone to that restaurant. Their food has progressively gotten worse."

"Stop the car *now*! Stop the dang car!" she screamed. She started foaming at the mouth, and the shaking got worse.

"We're on a busy two-lane road, sweetheart."

Katherine began to open her door, trying to push against the force of the wind.

"Whoa! Whoa! Hold on, honey!"

Their daughter, Mikala, yelled, "Mom, stop, we're still moving!"

Their son, Jade, frantically screamed, "Mom! No, Mom!"

Keith turned on his flashers and began to slow down. Cars behind him were continuously blowing their horns.

Just before the car came to a complete stop, Katherine jumped out and ran into the opposite lane of moving traffic. Jade jumped out and was trying to grab her when they were both struck by an SUV, which was then hit by a sedan. Katherine died instantly.

Police surrounded and blockaded the scene, and EMTs loaded the boy into an ambulance. "Sir, can you explain to me what happened?" an officer asked Keith.

Keith was almost unable to speak but managed to give the officer the relevant details.

"Did your wife have a history of mental health problems?" the officer asked.

"No, sir, but she had seemed paranoid since taking our son to the beach last weekend." Looking at his daughter, Keith became very concerned for her. "Mikala! You OK, baby?"

She couldn't answer.

"Put her into the ambulance and check her," the officer said to an EMT. "I think she's in shock. Hurry! Take her to County Hospital. Keith, would you like someone to drive you there?"

"I'm able, Officer."

"All right. The investigation team is here now. They'll finish up."

Keith and Katherine's son died later at the hospital.

* * *

In Boston, Massachusetts, the owner of a security company, Quinson Wade, was throwing his fifty employees a celebration for their outstanding performance in the prior quarter. The celebration was held at his penthouse, which was on the fiftieth floor.

"While I was doing some river rafting in Rock Springs, Wyoming, during my vacation, I was trying to think of ways to show my deepest appreciation for your devotion and hard work. I decided to have this event and to share with each of you the fruits of your labor. I would like for each of you to come to the table out on the balcony, take one envelope each, then come back in."

They all did as he instructed and stood before him as he went to the table and turned to face them.

"If you will open your envelopes, you'll each find ten one-hundred-dollar bills. And again, I say thanks to each of you."

His employees noticed that his speech was slurred, and he had begun shaking. He turned and walked to the balcony, raised both his hands, and tumbled over the brick-and-iron rail, falling to his death.

It was later revealed by his secretary that he had gone to see his doctor for the condition, as well as migraine headaches. He also had a green discoloration of his feet, all the way up to his ankles.

* * *

In Dallas, Texas, a fire chief was speaking with his lieutenant, Aston Mayo, who was also a scoutmaster and had just returned from a scouting expedition at Lake Texoma to confirm five Eagle Scouts.

"Well, Lieutenant, how'd things go at the camp?" the chief asked.

"Great, Chief. The boys were excited and couldn't wait to meet the challenges of their new rank. They're a great troop. I always enjoy being around them, and to see them accomplishing their short-term goals reassures me that their long-term goals are theirs for the taking. These kids are hard workers and ambitious."

"Lieutenant, you getting enough rest?"

"Sure thing, why do you ask, sir?"

"Oh, I don't know. You seem different somehow, and your eyes look tired, maybe a little droopy, even."

"I don't feel as though anything's wrong, but I could use a little more sleep. Being with kids for a whole week can wear on an old fellow!"

"Old? Yeah, just wait till you reach my age."

"Heck, I'll probably be retired and in a wheelchair by then."

"I'm not as old as you think."

"You're not? OK."

"What was the agenda for the five Eagle Scouts?"

"The usual—recite pledges and rules, prove survival skills and rescue skills, and take their Red Cross test again, with weights this time."

While Lieutenant Aston was changing from his shoes to his firehouse boots, the chief noticed the greenish appearance of his feet.

"Did you mash some green grapes for wine while you were gone as well?"

"No. Why would you ask that, sir?"

"Aww . . . pay me no mind, son. It's nothing."

It was Lieutenant Aston's first day back at work, and they received an alarm from downtown at an old warehouse.

"Lieutenant, you look beat. Why don't you cover the firehouse this time?" the chief asked.

"Come on, Chief. I got this. I'm OK."

Halfway to the warehouse, the truck turned a corner, and the lieutenant's eyes rolled to the back of his head. He almost lost his grip on the rear of the truck, but he came around.

When they arrived at the location, the chief barked orders: "Let's get hooked up, guys. The fire is spreading to the upper floors fast. Get the ladder out and up to the second floor. Check for trapped victims. Lieutenant, ride the ladder to the second floor."

"I'm on it, Chief."

When Lieutenant Aston reached the second floor, the chief's voice came over his radio: "Do you see any movement or anyone down?"

"Not from here. Too much flame. Need to get a closer look."

"You're too close now! Lieutenant, that's a negative!"

"I don't feel the flames, Chief. It's not too hot."

"*What?* Negative, Lieutenant! Back away and lower that boom! Now! That's an order!"

The lieutenant stepped off the ladder and walked through the burning open window.

The chief yelled to a firefighter, "Get another boom up there! Cover him with water, quick, until we get him lowered."

Before the firefighter could get the second boom in place, an explosion blew through the open second-floor window.

"Get that boom down! Darn it! I knew something wasn't right with him. It's my fault. We've lost him because I made a terrible decision," the chief said.

"Chief, I beg to differ. I saw the whole thing. Lieutenant made the decision."

"No, that decision was made at the firehouse. I let him come against my better judgment."

"Do you believe something was wrong with him? He had no regard or respect for the flames. Did he think he was invincible or what?" the firefighter asked.

"I don't know, but we'll get to the bottom of it, or it'll be my badge and my career!"

* * *

A couple who lived in Houston, Texas, was at a seafood restaurant that extended about fifty yards off land over the edge of a lake. While waiting to be seated, the husband and another customer started a conversation about visiting rivers in the Amazon to catch exotic fish—fish that had canines like dogs or lions, fish that could eat a person. The customer asked if he had ever been there before.

"Yeah, I just got back to Texas yesterday, and it was a memorable experience, to say the least," the husband said.

"Tell me, how did your trip come about?"

"Well, I was in that bait store on the other side of this restaurant, talking to the owner's son about some of those strange-looking fish that are hanging all over the store. He told me he and his father caught them all. I asked who caught the hammerhead, and he said he did, and I was like, 'Yeah, right,' and he said, 'No, really, I did,' and told me he was going to the Amazon in Brazil. His father had planned to go with him, but something pressing came up, so the son said he had a ticket and accommodations for two already paid for. I asked if he might consider selling his dad's ticket to me, and he agreed."

"Just like that, it was a done deal?"

"Oh no, I had to have the money the next day, and I did. Then it was a done deal. We were there for two days before we went out to this rain forest whose water was fed in from the mountains by the sea. It started out being a rough day because our small canoe got caught up in some strange-looking seaweed, and we had to get out of the boat and free it from the weeds. I was hoping I didn't get eaten by any strange fish."

"Man, I bet that was uncomfortable."

"You can't imagine! My feet were wet for the rest of the day and stunk like hell. When I showered, they looked as though I'd dyed them olive green."

"Good thing you didn't catch something deadly—or something deadly didn't catch you."

"Sorry, man, my table is ready. Nice talking with you!"

"Yeah, later, man. Have a good dinner."

"You too. Be good now."

Toward the end of dinner, the husband's wife asked if he was OK. "Hon, you've been just staring at those shish kebab sticks for five minutes. What's special about them? I wish you still stared at me that way."

He continued to stare at the shish kebabs.

"Hon, did you hear me?"

"You see how someone stuck these sticks through my shrimp? I wonder if the shrimp could feel it."

"You sure you're OK? What's that all about? Shish kebab sticks hurting the dead shrimp? Be for real."

"I'll bet you a thousand dollars the shrimp felt it."

He immediately stuck one of the shish kebab sticks about two inches into his left eye. He didn't even scream. He just got up and walked out of the restaurant.

Three waiters ran him down and held him while an ambulance was called.

* * *

A young man named Alfred Aldridge worked for the phone company in Waterbury, Connecticut, and was a union steward. Every Friday after work, Alfred would drive to the beach for the weekend and just sit on the beach wall and hang his feet into the ocean. As cold as it was, it didn't matter to Alfred. It was just his thinking time.

His coworkers began to believe that all the stress and bickering and fighting for employees' jobs was getting to him. He had become more and more distant from everyone. One of his friends noticed discoloration of his feet one day when he visited Alfred out of concern. Alfred said that he wasn't stressed at all.

Ray, Alfred's friend, asked him, "Then how do you explain that you don't even ask me to go to lunch anymore? We used to go every other Thursday."

"I don't know what to tell you. What do you want me to say, Ray?"

"Man, I know something's bothering you. Just tell me what I can do to help. You know I will."

Alfred's condition worsened, and by 5:00 p.m. that day, he had become paranoid.

When Alfred got off work the next day, he went to the covered garage, got into his car he had parked on the sixth level, started it, and just hammered on the accelerator. His car hit the retaining rails and bent them. He backed up and did it again.

The garage security guard called the police, who were only one block away, and they were there in less than five minutes. As the officers approached the garage, they heard a loud crash and looked up to see Alfred's car plunging to the ground.

Alfred's car hit the rear of the squad car, and he was killed instantly. The officers were able to exit their car and make it clear of the crash.

CHAPTER
NINE

Meanwhile, there were people all over the world having similar experiences because they had come into contact with the affected waters. Therefore, Surgeon General Dr. Paul Aser ordered a team of research scientists to do tests to find similarities and report their findings to him. In the meantime, he had his assistant set up a holographic telepresence meeting with these scientists, along with biology professors, the director of the Institute for Human Infections and Immunity, the assistant secretary of the US Department of Health and Human Services, the director of the Centers for Disease Control and Prevention, the director of the Task Force on Infectious Disease Preparedness and Response, representatives of the Center for Biodefense, and environmental quality specialists from all over the world. Professor Dodds and Rina were also in attendance.

Dr. Aser started the meeting, saying, "Good morning, ladies and gentlemen. The task that we've been charged with is challenging, to say the least. But I am confident that with the expertise in this room, it is achievable. That being said, let's discuss what you have discovered at this point and what we'll do going forward."

Debra Deeds, a representative of the Office of the Surgeon

General, stated, "Based on reports that we've heard, the effects in all cases differ in some minor aspects but are the same overall."

"Please be more specific," Dr. Aser responded.

"Professor Dodds, can you please address that?" Debra Deeds asked.

"In most cases, people merely had hallucinatory experiences," Professor Dodds said. "In other cases, individuals experienced psychological disturbances, and they became extremely violent and dangerous. But all became paranoid and believed they were seeing things that were not real, and it cost them their lives."

"What is the most common factor?" Dr. Aser asked.

"A common factor we've determined is that all had come in close proximity to some body of water that connects to the oceans, seas, rivers, or lakes that have been contaminated by certain plant life of a seaweed type. Well, not exactly."

"Can you explain 'not exactly'?"

"Meaning that this plant resembles seaweed in its makeup, but it is totally toxic in specific stages. This weed has three stages of toxins. At its first stage, which is at its root and base, it's very dark green. This is a milder toxin that causes hallucinatory effects. At its second stage, it's lighter green and can cause paranoia and violence. But at its end, the third stage, the toxins are quite potent and can cause death."

"Can you nail down what species of weed or a definite location of its growth?" Dr. Aser asked.

"Herein lies the difficult task. The DNA is not like any seaweed or any other plant life known to man," Dr. Smith, another scientist, responded.

"Is it possible that this is an undiscovered form that could have been around forever that just had not been discovered until now?" Dr. Aser asked.

"That could be a possibility, but it's not likely," Dr. Smith responded.

"Why is that?" Dr. Aser asked.

"Well, sir, the fact that it can alter the pigmentation of the skin is a testament to its toxicity and its originality. If it had been around forever, someone at some time would have experienced it and noted it. This changes pigmentation to an olive green upon contact, wet or dry. That's highly unusual."

"Could it be something that we unknowingly produced through toxic waste, or some experiment gone wrong?" Dr. Aser asked.

"That is one idea we discussed, but we discounted it because these symptoms have not been recorded at any known labs," another scientist, Dr. Floyd said.

"So, people, are we back to square one?" Dr. Aser asked.

"Sir, we never left!" Dr. Floyd responded.

Dr. Aser closed the meeting by saying, "OK. Well, for now. But we can't give in to the results thus far, so let's not give up. We will meet again soon. Keep searching and stay in touch with each other. Thanks, everyone."

* * *

After months of testing, the top scientists had drawn a blank, while people all over the world were still suffering reactions with similar effects. Some were dying, and others were losing their minds by the tens of thousands, going stark mad!

After even more testing, the teams scheduled another meeting with the surgeon general to report their findings.

* * *

Shortly afterward, the research scientists met with Dr. Aser and President Turnkey. Dr. Aser introduced the team to the president and gave the floor over to Dr. Floyd, the team leader, to report the findings.

Dr. Floyd introduced himself and said, "At first, Mr. President, we thought it might be some sort of parasite. But after studying its DNA composition, we've found that it's an enzyme that comes from a historical biblically named plant called wormwood, which has the power to affect people in horrible but very different ways. We tested tens of dozens of people and found out that individuals were being affected differently based on their blood type, body size, gender, age, and ethnicity. In some cases, people died, and in other cases, they went into comas."

"Can you elaborate?" President Turnkey asked.

"Yes, sir, we can," Dr. Floyd responded. "We found that younger victims were affected the least and with a milder state of severity. Most of them became very nauseous, with temporary loss of memory.

"The elderly, however, mostly became comatose. Of those who had existing medical conditions, almost one hundred percent died. Of those who didn't, about thirty percent died, and sixty-six percent recovered from the coma after only a few days, with few lasting signs. Of those in between the young and the elderly, those who were obese had about a forty percent chance of survival.

"Now here's where it gets a bit strange, even spooky. Of those who survived, at least ninety-five percent had some exposure to some sort of church values or teachings. For those who did not, the ratio was reversed. Ninety-five percent did not survive, and the five percent who did had substantial brain cell destruction!"

"I had a meeting with some clergy representatives a while ago, and at least one agreed, to a degree, with that finding," President Turnkey responded. "Could it be that the real answer lies with something spiritual taking place? And would it have to do with prophecy or just moral spiritual teachings?"

"Sir, do you think we can sell that to the public?" Dr. Floyd asked.

"At this point, the public is apt to believe any findings. But we must be careful which explanation we try to sell. The political fallout could be devastating. It would be in our best interest to confine your findings to a more scientific nature."

"But, sir, that's only part of what makes our findings relevant."

"It's never been in our best interest to mix religion, political, and scientific reasoning."

"How can we separate our findings into either part and make them stand alone? They are all so intertwined that it's dangerous to try to make either stand on its own as a defining solution or reason—with all due respect, sir."

"Though I consider myself to be not just religious but a Christian by claim," President Turnkey said, "I'm still the top political figure in the world and must do what is necessary to portray compliance with policy. Separation of church ideas and state ideas is the top command! I've got to meet with my advisors and members of the cabinet to consider how to handle this very sensitive matter. Our priorities must remain our focus."

"Exactly what priorities are we to keep in focus, sir?"

"That of not leaning toward religious extremism."

"Sir, do you really believe telling the truth of our findings is religious extremism?"

"No, as a matter of fact, I don't—but our friends across the aisle will! And they will challenge us openly on the matter. And I guarantee you that will hurt us with the elections so close! Do what you must. I've got to address the public very soon concerning the problem and cure.

"Let's back up. I think you've nailed it down for now. Let's go with the parasite theory. It's sellable, with no backlash potential. And the public has a tendency to go with new discoveries a hundred percent of the time anyway. Strike up another number one in the name of science. But on the other hand, I'm not positively sold on the idea that blood type, weight, size, gender, or age could have any bearing on how people react to encountering whatever this substance is. Still, the idea of an undiscovered parasite is the way to go forward with public reporting until we can find a cure and make a case."

"But, sir, there is no foreseeable cure. It's as though it's a curse or a punishment on humankind for something. The effects are so different, it's impossible to nail down a universal antidote. All we can do is relieve the suffering of those who survive for as long as we can."

"On that note, ladies and gentlemen, this meeting is adjourned," President Turnkey said.

CHAPTER
TEN

Monday, February 3, 2042

President Turnkey set up a meeting with the special task force he had put together to investigate all the strange events since 2038. This group was made up of a list of professionals invited from around the globe, which included Rev. Dr. Donald Mason, Mike T. Lathan Jr., Professor Clarence Dodds, and Rina Adelstein. The meeting took place at the World Health Organization headquarters in Geneva, Switzerland.

The president approached the podium and began to speak. "Good morning to each one of you. I would like to first thank all of you for accepting my invitation to be part of this very special and important task force. It is unique in many ways. We have gathered from around the world some of the most prominent clergies and some of the best scientists and medical doctors. Among them are representatives of the US Office of the Surgeon General. We are graced to have a specialized agency of the United Nations concerned with international public health, with leaders from other regional offices.

"I am thankful for your participation and your concern. There have been some strange events over the past few years, some related to weather and some not. Our purpose for coming together is to perform this task force's title: FOWGO—figure out what's going on!

"We have here today a wide variety of individuals who have had firsthand dealings with these events. We'll hear their stories in brief detail and will have opportunities to ask questions. I strongly suggest that no one be interrogated by any means. We want to hear facts so that they can be analyzed by each of you. We'll hear the experts in each field of concern give their interpretations of what they hear.

"I strongly advise everyone to take notes, if necessary, so that there will be no misunderstanding of facts. We have interpreters to ease some of the language barriers that may exist.

"First, we want to hear from celebrated professor of science Dr. Clarence Dodds, who has had much interaction with the White House Office of Science and Technology Policy. Professor Dodds, please activate your mic and begin."

"Thank you, Mr. President." Professor Dodds said. "It is my privilege, sir. I recently gave a lecture on how modern science is just new discoveries of the preexisting. I dismissed class when one of my students, who is with me today, heard a strange pounding on the roof, and we went to a window in the science lab to see something certainly new to our generation, even our millennium. We saw what appeared to be balls of burning ice falling from the sky, and when they made contact with the ground, grass, and trees, all manner of vegetation burst into flames. We could see the balls striking cars, buildings, homes, and other structures, yet no damage occurred.

He continued. "Rina, my student, and I went outside after the downpour ceased some forty-five minutes later. As we surveyed what was happening, most of the balls took about twenty minutes to, shall I say, melt themselves out. We were able to get some samples, which didn't last. Heck, we didn't know whether to freeze them or simply hold them in little metal containers. It didn't matter, though, because none lasted more than twenty minutes. So there was not much to study—no ice, no blood, only a stone that appeared to be nothing less or more than a rock of granitelike composition, which, over a short period of time, actually dissolved to nothing, not even dust. Just gone!

"Hours later, I walked into the lab where we had stored some of the hail, and there was nothing. The containers were empty, leaving no trace of anything. Some have said that the burning hail that fell in Egypt came to the same end. No trace of any type of substance or residue. Our constant research has led us to the same dead end: that this has not been recorded happening for approximately some thirty-six hundred years, according to Thutmose III Bible archaeology. Some sources would even say it was approximately forty-six hundred years. If either is correct, we can all agree that it's not a common occurrence. But this is all we have to go on, except we found out that people who came into contact with these balls of burning ice were, in fact, burned rather severely."

Everyone there seemed to be mesmerized by his account.

"So is there anything anyone can add?" President Turnkey asked.

Mike raised his hand.

"Yes, sir, Mr. Lathan, am I correct?"

"That is correct, Mr. President."

"Do you have a question or comment? Please take the mic."

"An observation of a record, sir."

"You may proceed."

"Some of our Holy Bible's subject headings would describe the burning hail that fell upon Egypt during the pharaoh's reign as a plague, which suggests that it was punishment for the Egyptians. Could it be that man is being punished?"

"Punished for what?"

"There are, if we believe the Holy Bible to be factual, a few possibilities."

"Can you elaborate more?"

"There is a worldwide spread of hate among people of different nations, cultures, races, and economic status. A clear contradiction of what is commanded in the Scriptures."

"Do you truly believe there is an acceptable fix for hatred? You know that the hardest thing to change about a man is what he was raised to believe to be true."

"Well, that's why I believe there is a fix, but it's not one that would be accepted. In essence, there is no possible fix, sir."

"Then there may not be hope for humanity if the words recorded in the Bible are true, because science does not have enough evidence to prove otherwise."

"Unless, of course, someone does but, for some reason, is not sharing their discovery!"

"If there is nothing more to be discussed or brought out concerning this strange, historical hail occurrence, we'll move on to the next topic."

Nothing more was voiced concerning the hail, so the president moved forward. "Now let's shift our attention to the next item to be discussed. We'll start by hearing from naval Executive Officer Tom Powell. Please activate your mic and begin."

"First and foremost, I thank you, Mr. President," Executive Officer Powell began. "I am first mate to Captain August Brown aboard the USS *Fight*, a recon vessel deployed to the north central region of the Pacific Ocean.

"On March 30, 2040, I went to the deck to check on how the weather seemed to be trending. While looking toward the sunrise, I heard a very loud boom. I asked one of the deck sailors if he heard anything, but he didn't. It sounded to me like the sound barrier being broken. I couldn't understand why no one else had heard it.

"I grabbed my binoculars that I had around my neck and scanned the northern skies. I saw movement behind what appeared to be morning haze. It looked like a mountain falling from the sky, and it seemed to disappear into the ocean, at least twenty-five miles away, maybe farther.

"About an hour and a half later, we began receiving distress signals from hundreds of vessels—large, small, private, and military—ours and international. They were being pulled by some unexplainable force toward the same area. After more time passed, we too began to be pulled in that direction. Captain Brown allowed us to be drawn in until our radar tech gave him a report that this mysterious force that was drawing us in seemed to be a whirling vortex in the ocean of about some three to four and a half miles in diameter, with a tunnel of nearly thirty to forty miles. We later learned that we were caught in a seemingly inescapable pull when hearing of hundreds of ships and boats being drawn to their destruction. The captain commanded all our power be shifted to reverse, and we were able to pull free.

"But many vessels weren't powerful enough to break free and met a horrifying end. While circling at a safe distance of about five miles from the force of the pull, we saw many who could not escape the force being drawn past us. We went into rescue mode and were able to pick up some who survived, their vessels already sunken and destroyed. The number of ships and bodies we witnessed was totally disheartening."

"How long did you stay in rescue mode?" President Turnkey asked.

"Until the next daybreak, when we were ordered to return to home port with the survivors we already had."

"Anyone have questions for Executive Officer Powell?" President Turnkey asked.

A United Nations representative from the Western Pacific Region asked, "How is it that you were able to pull free when others could not?"

"Ma'am, our vessel, the USS *Fight*, is one of the most powerful crafts known. It exceeds thirteen thousand four hundred horsepower."

The president, in an effort to close the meeting, looked at his watch and said, "The morning has been far spent, and I'd like to thank each of you for your input. However, I would like to recommend that we break for lunch and meet back here in ninety minutes. When we return, we'll try to move a little faster to close out this meeting, hopefully with some sort of plan. There are several restaurants within this compound. I strongly suggest that no one exit the premises. See you all back here in an hour and a half."

As Mike and Rev. Dr. Mason made their way to lunch, Mike saw Rina enter a restaurant with Professor Dodds. Professor Dodds recognized Rev. Dr. Mason, and they greeted each other. Rina looked in Mike's direction—just the opportunity he had been waiting for. He had not been able to take his eyes off her since before the meeting started.

Mike approached Rina and introduced himself. "Hello, I'm Michael T. Lathan Jr. And you are . . ."

"Rina Adelstein. What is your field, Michael T. Lathan Jr.?"

"I recently received my master's in divinity, with a minor in science. I work for a science and engineering research laboratory in Dallas, Texas. How about you?"

"I'm a senior science student at the University of Washington in Seattle."

"I'm very familiar with Professor Dodds's reputation as one of our most celebrated scientists and professors. I've admired his work over the years."

"Professor Dodds often speaks of a bright young scientist who, if he focused on his scientific research, could be great. I believe his name is Michael T. Lathan Jr., scientist slash preacher. Could that be you?"

"One and the same."

"Wow, I feel as though I've known you for at least three years, yet I don't know much about you."

"You could learn more about me if you'd like. Please allow me to buy your lunch. I promise I'll get us back on time. Dr. Mason, do you mind if I—"

Cutting in before he finished his request, Rev. Dr. Mason answered, "Not at all, Mike, you go right on ahead. I'll see you later, OK?"

"Hold on. I haven't agreed yet!" Rina said. "Professor, is it OK with you if I accompany Mr. Lathan for lunch?"

"Sure, you two youngsters have a good lunch, and we'll meet you both here later," Professor Dodds responded.

Rina and Mike ordered lunch, but neither ate much. They were both desperately trying to get to know each other. It appeared to be love at first sight. Although both tried too hard to hide it, both felt it.

The meeting reconvened exactly ninety minutes after the start of lunch.

President Turnkey approached the podium and said, "Will everyone please move quickly back to your seats? We have a lot to discuss in a short period. I don't want anyone to miss their shuttles to the airport or hotels. Thank you for your cooperation.

"I would like to, at this time, yield the floor to Dr. Murray Murphy, physician and practitioner in the Canary Islands. You may activate your mic, Dr. Murray. Good afternoon. I hope that you're well."

"Thank you, Mr. President. I am well, sir." Dr. Murphy responded.

"Doctor, it is recorded that you treated a man who apparently had encountered some sort of hallucinatory substance that greatly affected his ability to communicate and perform in the reality of his surroundings. What is your interpretation of his condition?"

"Sir, he seemed quite normal in every way until he spoke. Then it was as if he was in a fantasy world of his own, where he saw and spoke with human skeletons as though they were normal conversations. He came to my office and saw a skeletal model hanging on a hook and told his brother that he had just seen that fellow on the beach eating dead people. He was quite serious.

"When I examined him visually, I saw a greenish tint on his feet. His blood work revealed a substance that was proven to be a highly toxic substance from ancient times called wormwood. It's thought to have been the cause of great calamities in earlier times. It has been discovered growing in desolate places in several parts of the world. The common name for it is *Artemisia absinthium*, and it gives off a bitter oil with an aromatic smell. One chemical found in it is thujone, which is potentially very poisonous and can be deadly. I've treated several patients who have come into contact with this chemical. Some have died, and others are still comatose. How the first patient encountered it when walking in the waters of a North African beach is yet another mystery.

"There are over eighty species of this plant that can be found in Europe and Asia and now in North America."

A World Health Organization representative then requested to speak. "Doctor, how could this chemical have been spread to so many different regions not common or hospitable to its growth?"

"Ladies and gentlemen, I have often pondered that very concern, especially the possibility of water supplies around the globe being infiltrated."

A hand went up, and a voice spoke out. "Mr. President and task force council, may I please speak?"

"Please activate your mic so that we can hear you clearly. And who might you be?" President Turnkey asked.

"Sir, I am Executive Officer Miguel Mendez, first mate to Captain Walter Wright aboard the USS *Washington-Goldwater*. While we were in a certain area, I heard a loud booming sound in the sky."

"Which ocean, Executive Officer Mendez?"

"The Atlantic, only a few hundred miles from shore. Mild waves rushed toward the shorelines, carrying all sorts of debris, forcing it toward the entrances of many of our main rivers. That water could have made it inland into rivers and lakes by underwater currents."

"That could be possible, but all around the globe, I'm not so sure," President Turnkey said.

A health council representative requested to speak and said, "It could be that this enormous splashdown could have caused currents to meet crosscurrents and diagonal currents that could cover thousands of miles in a few days."

"Is that logical?" President Turnkey asked.

"Sir, both logical and possible, and it is apparent that something quite unusual happened. People all around the world are still being affected."

"Mr. President," Dr. Quann, the director of environmental quality, said. "Might I remind everyone of all the coastal flooding on the continents in the path of the waves the splashdown caused. That could very well explain how main rivers may have been polluted by this oily chemical, because some have direct spill points into lakes and freshwater reservoirs."

"That's the only way it could have spread so widely so quickly. People all over the world are still being poisoned and dying. If we can do anything about it, it lies in the possibility of coming up with an antidote and a distribution scheme as fast as possible," President Turnkey said.

A United Nations representative spoke up. "Mr. President, extensive testing has been conducted on this strain, and it has been found to be twenty times more toxic than the strains tested in the past. The ability to create an effective antidote has proven to be quite the challenge."

"I have confidence that together we can accomplish it," President Turnkey responded. "We have summoned the best scientists the world has to offer. Besides, annihilation of humankind is the only other option. Not on my watch! We will make it happen! Does anyone here believe that this may be the cause of the loss of sea life in such high numbers?

And second, we have the challenge to discover what could have turned so great a portion of ocean waters into a bloodlike substance. Anyone? We need some ideas here that make good sense or maybe good science. Rev. Dr. Mason, is that your hand I see? You have the floor, sir."

"Mr. President," Rev. Dr. Mason said. "I do believe that the possibility of chemical warfare is eliminated, because all nations are being affected. Has anyone besides some of the clergy considered that maybe, just maybe, there's something to indicate a fulfilled prophecy that is laid out in the Holy Bible? Nothing else can be proven. Actually, nothing else makes good sense!"

"Let's say that maybe there's truth to that. What will be the result? Or what may be the next calamity that we could face?" President Turnkey asked.

"Sir, as much as I believe it to be true, I would say that if it's what's next in the prophecy, none of us should look forward to it—unless, of course, the whole world accepts and embraces Christianity."

"It is a fact that Christianity has spread to most regions of the world."

"That is a fact for sure, but I mean to every heart in the world."

"That's probably not likely, being that there are so many other beliefs that are based on an experience with a higher deity."

"Then what is very likely to happen is that those who do not have God's mark when it occurs will wish—or shall I say, will beg—for the mark of God! Sir, I may add that no one unmarked will be able to escape the terror of what will come. I do believe that this generation is the generation to experience *it*!"

"Some would believe this generation will be far gone from this life by then."

"I wouldn't want to see it happen to any generation, but I'm just a messenger. I can't control the future."

A hand raised in the middle of the room.

"Yes, sir, you may speak," President Turnkey said.

"Sir, I'm a lab scientist, Dr. Collin Justin," he said. "I am assigned to the USS *Fight*. I personally tested the substance resembling blood and found it to be, in fact, blood. But the DNA is of a pattern I've never seen, and I was unable to match it with any known DNA pattern. There must be something more than science involved here. What that might be, I'm not able to determine."

"Might I remind everyone here that the purpose and title of the task force are one and the same: FOWGO. Finding Out What's Going On!

"I truly hope that we can get sound answers sometime soon," President Turnkey continued. "We owe it to our public, all of us. To those of us who believe that we answer to a higher power, whoever or whatever it may be, let us stay prayerful for answers. To those who have other beliefs, lean on them a little harder until enlightenment comes."

Coming to no apparent conclusions that would support the task force's title, the president ended the meeting.

"Thank you for your time and dedication. Look to meet again soon. Good day to all and thanks to everyone. Goodbye! You're dismissed!"

On Mike's way out, he desperately looked for Rina, who was hoping that he would. Just as he passed the ladies' restroom, he saw her enter.

He said to Rev. Dr. Mason, "I'll meet you back at the hotel. I've got to see her before I leave."

"She is a beauty. I can't blame you at all. We're not leaving until tomorrow afternoon, so good luck!"

"Thanks, I'll need it. I think I—"

"Don't say it unless you mean it."

"I know and I do."

"Well, I believe that's the way it's supposed to happen."

After a few minutes, Rina exited the restroom and saw Mike with a lost look on his face.

"I hoped to see you again before we left Geneva," Rina said.

"Probably not as much as I hoped for it. Let's exchange contact information." And they did.

"I'm in school in Washington and my part-time job doesn't pay much, but I'll do what I can to see you again."

"I live in Dallas in a division called Highland Park."

"What, are you serious? My brother lives in Dallas in a small community called Arlington Park. Do you know where it is?"

"It's only about a ten-minute drive from where I live. If I can get you there for Thanksgiving, my mother's favorite holiday, will you come?"

"I'm a good old-fashioned girl, so I must OK it through my parents, especially my father—he's very protective—and my brother, who's more protective of me than my parents. But at least he'd love to have dinner with me then. He is invited, isn't he?"

"Of course he is. By the way, I'd love to meet your parents and have you meet mine."

"Whatever it takes to see you again, I'll do it."

Rina did not get a chance to spend Thanksgiving with Mike that year. However, over the next few years, they became closer through video calls, emails, and texts.

CHAPTER
ELEVEN

November 2044
Thanksgiving Day

The doorbell rang. Mrs. CheRee Lathan looked through the peephole and said, "Hallelujah! God's still working miracles!"

"Who is it, sweetheart? It's got to be Mike, with that kind of jubilance!" Rev. Dr. Michael T. Lathan Sr. asked.

"My baby still loves his mom's cooking! Looks like he's lost some weight since we last saw him. Well, we're gonna take care of that little problem today." Mrs. Lathan, opening the door, said, "We were beginning to think you'd forgotten where we live."

"I've missed you both as well, Mom."

"Come on in, son. Sweetheart, take his coat," his father said,

"I don't think he's forgotten where the closet is. Have you, Mike? It's been a while," Mrs. Lathan said.

"Uncle, uncle; I give, I give. I'm patting the mat three times already!"

"A simple 'I'm sorry, Mom and Dad' will do just fine. Maybe it won't be so long next time," Rev. Dr. Lathan responded.

"OK, OK! I'm terribly sorry. I'll do better. Knowing my mother, I'm sure dinner has been ready since lunch."

"Try since before breakfast. Your mother's been just too excited since you told me you were looking forward to being here."

"Truth is, I haven't had a well-rounded meal in a while."

"Why? We taught you how to eat healthy," Mrs. Lathan said.

"I know, it's on me. I've let my work and my research cause me to resort to fast food for quite some time."

"You know you're welcome to eat here three meals a day, seven days a week, fifty-two . . ."

Dr. Lathan cried, "Hold on, that's enough! I didn't send him through college for six years for him to make this his free buffet!"

"Apologize to your son this very moment!"

"We're like this, aren't we, son?" he asked, raising his index finger and placing it over his heart and then his head.

"Don't get alarmed, Mom. It's a father-and-son thing. I know where he's coming from."

An hour later, sitting at the dinner table, Dr. Lathan asked Mike, "Will you give God honor by asking for His blessings over dinner? You do still know how to, right?"

"Dad, don't you start."

Mike got even. He prayed for five whole minutes. After he finished, Mrs. Lathan said, "You did that, hon!"

"Still a maverick, are you?" Dr. Lathan responded.

After dinner, Mike and his father moved into the study to talk.

"Tell me, son, have you given any consideration to the offer I proposed to you? I'm getting old, as you know," Rev. Dr. Lathan said.

"I'm still trying to see where things are headed. A lot has been going on for the last few years. I've been wrapped up in research."

"A lot of what? And how does that affect you coming to church every Sunday and assuming the role as assistant to the pastor?"

"A lot has been going on with the weather the last four years.

Rev. Dr. Mason and I have been trying to find a connection between the prophecy and global warming."

"Michael T. Lathan Jr., are you serious? Really? I thought your research was centered on new species of something or another, or the moon, stars."

"This is the twenty-first century, Dad. The world's problems are a lot greater than those. We've got to keep up!"

"I'm not asking you to be the assistant pastor, Mike, but rather to assist your father. I could really use your input and your legs."

"It's a great opportunity, I know, but I can't be that committed. It will take me away from my research. Dad, I love you dearly, so please give me time to cool the irons. I've got a lot going on already that I need to sort out before I can put any more into the fire."

"I owe you that much, son. I hope I'm still alive by the time you make up your mind. Besides, the entire Methodist Conference is waiting for the second Dr. Michael T. Lathan to assume the mantle!"

"Anyway, Dr. Mason has invited me to accompany him to several meetings. I've also been invited to attend some seminars and have accepted some speaking engagements."

"Well, I don't think I can interfere with such important stuff, but is it more important than assisting your dad?"

"Dad, really, how could . . . Never mind. Why would you make me choose between my passion and yours? You've always taught me to be my own man. I'm trying to be just that. That doesn't mean I don't love you."

Mrs. Lathan knocked on the door and entered.

"OK, boys! That's enough business time. Let's enjoy some family time and listen to some seasonal songs and music."

They all went into the family room to do so. The evening became far spent and night fell. "Well, I hate to run, but I've got to get an early start tomorrow," Mike said.

"Son, I wish you would rest tomorrow. Let your food have time to digest and give your body and mind time to reset," Mrs. Lathan said.

"Take your mom's advice. The moon, sun, and stars will be there the next day," Dr. Lathan added.

"The way things are going, there's no guarantee of that at all. Good night. I love you both."

CHAPTER
TWELVE

Friday before Thanksgiving, November 17, 2045

After three years of developing a close relationship, Mike and Rina decided to spend Thanksgiving with his parents. Rina received a call.

"Hello, Mike, how are you?"

"Good morning. I am much better now that I've heard your voice."

"Oh my, that was expected."

"I beg your pardon?"

"My brother warned me to be on guard for those kinds of lines."

"Remind me to thank him, will you? He ruined my best approach for starting a great day."

"Just joking, Mike. My brother was the kind of guy I'm afraid of. He was the true example of trouble before he got married."

"Please don't scare me like that. I was totally at a loss for words. By the way, I'm just calling to confirm next week's visit."

"My parents gave their consent, and my brother says he has plans but wishes me to have a good time. I received my round-trip ticket, and I will be on the flight. Mike, you really shouldn't have, but I'm so very glad that I'll get a chance to spend Thanksgiving with you. I made plans to stay with my brother for a few days afterward."

"Well, my parents are anxious to meet the woman who has stolen their son's heart."

"They must know that it's my heart that has been taken captive."

"Then I will pick you up at Dallas Love Field Airport this coming Wednesday."

"Yes, I'll be there. I'll call you before my flight takes off."

"When your flight lands, just look out the window. I'll be the lovesick one standing at the end of the runway."

"Won't that be dangerous? Will security even allow it?"

"No! They won't! But I will be at your gate waiting."

"Why do I think you just toyed with my mind? Well, at least it wasn't my heart."

"To toy with your heart would be to deceive my own. It was merely the expression of my deepest desire to see you."

"Though I couldn't have expressed it so metaphorically, my desires to see you are as anxious. I will see you then. Goodbye."

"Yes, uh . . . OK . . . I'll see you then. Goodbye."

* * *

On the day before Thanksgiving, Rina's flight landed at Dallas Love Field Airport.

"Ma'am, please stay seated until we come to a complete stop. You look as though someone special is waiting for you," the flight attendant said.

"Someone very special indeed," Rina agreed.

"Such a lucky girl! Wow!"

"I'm blessed and I'm so happy!"

As soon as Rina walked through the gate, she saw a tall, handsome figure with the expression of a little boy on Christmas morning seeing his very first bicycle. He just looked at her and smiled.

"Mike, are you OK?"

"I wish you could feel just how OK I am right now."

"I do. Believe me when I say I do. Do we have time to swing by my brother's home?"

"Of course, plenty of time. It's only five minutes from here. Give me his address and I'll just google it. Baggage claim is this way."

After they had waited at baggage claim for twelve and a half minutes, Rina's luggage showed up. "There, those four are mine, the pink-and-blue ones," Rina said as she spotted her bags.

"How long did you say you're staying at your brother's?"

"Oh, come on, not that long. I called him, and he had an emergency at his job and won't be home for about three hours. He asked me to let him know when I arrive at his house, and he will let me in."

"Well, if you wish, we can go directly to my parents' home. They're expecting to see you today anyway."

"I hope I'm not being a bother."

"If I know my mom, she'll offer you her guest room. She'll probably insist that you stay, at least until Amir gets home."

"Let's see what your mother has to say first. Oh, and let me contact my parents and let them know I arrived, OK?"

"Sure, go right ahead."

Twenty minutes later, they arrived at the Lathans' home in Highland Park. Mike used his key and opened the door.

Mrs. Lathan greeted them in the living room. "Good afternoon, my dear, come right in. Oh my, Mike, she's gorgeous!"

"You're too kind. You're making me blush. Ma'am, I've heard so much about you."

"Not nearly as much as I've heard about you, I guarantee."

"Mom, please don't embarrass me now. Where's Dad? Is he here?"

"Yes, he's in his study. I'll get him."

"Don't bother. I'll get him."

He knocked on his father's study door. Dr. Lathan opened it. "Mike, come on in, son."

"Dad, I want you to meet Rina."

"Hello, sir. I'm Rina Adelstein, daughter of Aryeh Adelstein, my father, and Shiran Adelstein, my mother."

"I'm very pleased to meet you, young lady; lady, indeed. Wow! An old-fashioned girl, so rare nowadays. It's refreshing to see young people who pay so much homage to their parents. There's hope for society yet."

"If it's OK with you and Mom, her brother won't be home for a while, so can she relax here?"

"By all means. Let me show you where you can refresh yourself and relax," Mrs. Lathan offered.

"I am so filled with gratitude, ma'am," Rina replied.

"Please, call me CheRee."

"But my parents would not approve; it's not proper."

"As you wish. Mike, I like her already! Are you hungry, dear? I know you've had a lengthy flight."

"Maybe later—I had a snack on the plane."

"*Snack?* Mike, you told me you flew her first class!" Dr. Lathan said.

"Sir, I did fly first class. I just wasn't hungry. I guess I was so excited about meeting you both, maybe even a little nervous."

"We're equally as excited to meet you. Mike's not quite been the same since he met you. I can see why. Not only are you beautiful, but you seem so well rounded. What do you do?"

"Well, I recently graduated from the University of Washington in Seattle as a science major, and I work at the school in the research lab as a science technician. I am a Christian, foremost."

"And her priorities are definitely in order, Mike."

"Dad . . ."

"Just making an observation, not an insinuation. But now that you brought it up, we'll discuss it further later."

"Thanks," Mike replied. "Mom, maybe you can introduce Rina to some old-fashioned American holiday cooking. Cooking is such a part of the holiday season in almost all American homes, Rina."

"In our country and our culture as well. My mother learned from her mother, who learned from her mother, and so on, for generations upon generations."

"And how about you?" Mrs. Lathan asked.

"I'm a scientist so far, but I'm still willing to learn to cook."

Dr. Lathan waved his arms and said, "Mike! Code red! Just kidding around, OK? I'm not like that. We went through learning curves, didn't we, dear?"

"Don't listen to him, you two. He's always loved my cooking. Most of dinner has already been prepared, but there are still a few dishes and desserts we can work on," Mrs. Lathan said.

Later that evening, Mike took Rina to her brother's, and they spent a couple of hours with him.

Rina spent Thanksgiving Day with Mike and his parents at their home. They had a memorable evening and a dinner they would never forget. After spending the rest of the weekend with her brother and occasionally with Mike, Rina had to depart for home in Seattle because her job awaited.

CHAPTER
THIRTEEN

December 2045

Upon reporting back to work at the school lab, Rina had messages to call a friend whom she went to college with at the University of Washington who now worked as a Program Coordinator/Volcanologist for the US Geological Survey Volcano Hazards Program at the Department of the Interior in Reston, Virginia.

"Hello, Misty, or shall I say, 'Dr. Myers'? How've you been, lady? I haven't spoken to you since graduation," Rina said.

"It has been a while, seemingly forever, Professor Adelstein. Girl, have you gotten out of that lab long enough to meet Mr. Right?" Misty asked.

"Well, since my new position as science professor over at the lab, I have been doing some travel research. Do you remember Professor Dodds?"

"Of course! I also remember that you were the professor's—or shall I say the teacher's—pet. He was very high on you. So what's going on with you nowadays?"

"Slow down the pace, lady. That's a lot of info you're requesting, some quite private."

"I knew it. You've met someone, haven't you? Come on, don't fib. Give me the juice!"

"Back up a step. First of all, I don't live in the lab. I just work there, and my work is fun."

"It's not often one can make a living and enjoy it. Stop dancing around the roses. I know you've picked a nice one."

"Well, if you must know, I met the most wonderful man. He lives in Dallas, Texas."

"Rina, what in heaven's name were you doing in Texas?"

"I don't know if you remember my brother, Amir, but he lives there."

"How convenient!"

"That's not where I met Mike. I was invited to a meeting in Geneva, Switzerland, by Professor Dodds to discuss some of the strange happenings that started in 2038. I was preparing to leave after three days there, and I saw the most beautiful set of green eyes looking at me. I was totally mesmerized. Neither of us knew what to say, but both of us wanted to say something. He got the nerve to break the stares first, and I'm just so blessed to meet him. I spent this past Thanksgiving with him and his parents and my brother, and it was heavenly!"

"Whoa, girl, sounds like it won't be long before you get married. Wait! You're not married yet, are you?"

"No, not yet! But with him, I'm definitely thinking of it. But I know you didn't call to see if I'm hitched yet. What's going on?"

"Well, I know science has been one of your passions, so how would you like to share some of your genius with me?"

"I don't understand."

"Well, speaking of strange occurrences . . . Rina, there's been some even stranger things being reported to our office from places like Yellowstone National Park, Cotopaxi National Park, and many,

many more. These places have been monitoring not only volcano activity but also the Earth's core, which is seemingly rising toward the surface at a very slow pace, but that pace appears to be speeding up."

"That's been happening over centuries, so what's strange about it now?"

"There's no clear reason—no temperature changes, no pressure buildup. As a matter of fact, it appears to be boring or drilling its own path."

"What? How can that be? What evidence is there to support that?"

"That's what's strange. There is no support, no proof, but the caves seem to be moving upward. Not always straight up but upward for sure. Even where you are by Mount Saint Helens, there appears to be movement."

"At my office, we've picked up some small tremors and light shifting of plates, but nothing out of the ordinary. My friend—"

"Mike, first-name-basis Mike, right?"

"Yes, that Mike, first-name-basis Mike is Rev. Dr. Michael T. Lathan's son."

"Rina, the Rev. Dr. Michael T. Lathan Sr.? The well-known preacher?"

"One and the same! He's also a scientist with strong knowledge in geology."

"Would the both of you think about coming to Reston to do some brainstorming based on the data I've collected over the past few months?"

"Personally, I think Mike would love the challenge, and so would I. I could invite him to come along, but I think he'd be more excited if the invite came from your office."

"OK then, give me his contact information, and I'll contact him about it. Then I'll get back to you with his response."

"If I know him well enough, you won't have to get back to me. He'll be too excited not to call me."

"OK, girl, let's do this sometime after the first of the year. It'll take me that much time to set the arrangements."

"Great, let's do it, then. I can't wait. I'm sure Professor Dodds and the school will agree that it'll be worth the trip."

March 2046

Mike received a call.

"Hello."

"Dr. Michael T. Lathan Jr.?"

"Yes, this is Dr. Michael T. Lathan Jr."

"I am Dr. Misty Myers, a friend of Rina's."

"Rina Adelstein?"

"Yes, Professor Rina Adelstein."

"She told me you would call me. And yes, I'd love to join your brainstorming session in July—or, shall I say, your session of the brains."

"You flatter me, but don't stop. I discussed with Rina some of the strange activity that's been happening around the Ring of Fire. Are you familiar with it?"

"Yes, I've done some study in the areas of the Ring of Fire as a subject, but I've done more extensive research on volcanoes and their origins."

"Well, this would probably interest you very much because of what seems to be occurring."

"What time frame are you looking at?"

"I can have all my data ready for evaluation and discussion by mid-June."

"OK then, I'll set my schedule to keep that time frame open."

"I've spoken with Rina a few times. She's just waiting for you to respond so that she can set her scheduling as well. I'll give her all the specifics when I'm done, and I'll look forward to seeing both of you then, OK?"

"Yes, but I'm sure I'll see Rina before then," he said with a smile.

"OK, it's set. Rina and I will talk more as well. See you then. Goodbye."

"Have a great day. Goodbye."

Mike called Rina to let her know he had spoken with Misty and agreed to make the trip. He told her he would arrange for her to meet him at the Dallas Love Field Airport when the time came.

May 15, 2046
Seattle, Washington

Rina heard a knock on her office door. "Come in, please," she said.

Rina's secretary entered the room and said, "Someone is here to see you."

"Me? Send them in."

A deep, slow voice said, "Good morning, my lady."

"Mike!"

Rina rushed over, hugged him, and gave him a light kiss on his right cheek.

"Oh my, let me back out and reenter. Another one of those would definitely make my day!"

"What on earth are you doing here? Why didn't you call me? I would have picked you up at the airport."

"Oh, I rented a car. I wanted to surprise you. Happy birthday!"

"Mike, what a pleasant surprise. I didn't think you would remember. Where's my gift? Just kidding. I'm just happy to see you."

"As a matter of fact, I stopped by the mall and picked up a little something for you."

He handed her a box the size of a shoebox.

"How sweet of you, Mike."

She let out a scream that scared everyone, and they came running into her office.

"Mike—Mike! Wha-wha-what is this?"

"Since I met you, I've wanted to be a permanent part of your life and I've missed you so much, I can't breathe. You're the very air I breathe, Rina. Will you—"

"Yes! Yes! I will! I will! When? When? Right now, I will."

"OK, that wasn't quite what I expected, but let's make plans after we return from Reston in July."

"Mike, you've made me the happiest I've ever been. Waiting will be painful, knowing my joy is standing in front of me. Yes, I'll wait until July—not one minute later, you got it?"

Happy laughter and clapping filled the room while Mike slipped the engagement ring on her finger.

"It fits. How'd you know it would?"

"I've been communicating with Amir, and he gave me his approval. I hope your parents will as well."

"When they meet you, they'll love you. I have no doubt of that. To know you is to love you, and I do. But what about your parents, Mike?"

"They'll respect my desires. Heck, Mom already is calling you the daughter she's always wanted. Gotta watch Dad, though. He'll play with your mind, so don't let him intimidate you with his intellectualness. I want to take my fiancée to lunch. Can you wrap up what you're doing and give me some time? I did just fly 1,681 miles to see the woman I want to spend the rest of my life with. I'm buying."

They spent the rest of the day together, and then Mike flew back to Dallas. Afterward, they spent countless hours communicating via holographic calls every day.

CHAPTER
FOURTEEN

Tuesday, July 10, 2046

Rina's flight landed at Dallas Love Field Airport at 9:48 a.m., and Mike was there waiting. He informed her that his mother was preparing lunch.

When they arrived at the Lathans' home, they were greeted at the door by Dr. Lathan. "Well, well, come on in, happy people."

"Good morning, sir. Good morning, ma'am. I am a happy person, indeed," Rina said.

"Yes, dear, happiness is a prerequisite to being in a lifelong commitment," Mrs. Lathan said. "We're happy for the both of you. It's refreshing to see Mike wanting to begin a new life of sharing. He's been far too committed to his research. I'm glad he'll have something more definite to give himself to."

"Wow, Mom, I don't know if I even need to research that one," Mike said.

"Son," Dr. Lathan said, "all she's saying is that she's worried about your personal life. In a lab is not where we'd like to see you spend the majority of your time. Besides, we were beginning to wonder if we would be getting any grandchildren while we could still enjoy watching them grow up."

"Whoa, whoa, whoa! Before we can give you grand-anything, I've got to speak to her parents! She wants me to give her time to prepare them for an American son-in-law. Her brother married a young lady from their country. Maybe they were expecting the same from her. Nevertheless, she seems to think there'll be no problems. I'm planning to go there after the research meeting in Reston, Virginia."

"What research meeting?"

"Oh, I'm sorry. I haven't told you two about it yet, have I?"

"Mike! You know you haven't! What's going on?"

"Well, I've been invited to Reston for a meeting—or, if you will, a discussion slash brainstorming session. Around the Ring of Fire, there's been a systematic series of movements upward toward the Earth's surface from its core, unexplained by any clear evidence."

"Ring of Fire, as in the circle of volcanoes?" Mrs. Lathan asked.

"Yes, that's right. I don't have enough information to make a reasonable assumption as of yet, but there'll be a lot of experts there. We'll figure it out. Our flight leaves early in the morning."

"Where will you two be staying, and how long do you expect to be there?" she asked.

"Don't worry, Mom. We'll have different quarters. I'll be at the Hilton, and Rina will be staying with a friend who works at the office of the Geological Survey Volcano Hazards Program there in Reston. We're looking to be there for about ten to eleven days. I'll keep you updated about any interesting findings if there are any. But right about now, Rina should get some rest before the day is too far spent."

"Mike, show Rina to her room, please."

"Yes, Mom, I will. This way, Rina. Get as much rest as you need. I'll let you know when lunch is ready."

"Mike, will you please spend some time with me after lunch?"

Rina saw a look on Mrs. Lathan's face and added, "Uh, in the living room, of course."

"I'll be in Dad's study. Just let me know when you're ready, OK?"

"OK, see you in a little while."

Rina rested for a little over an hour. Meanwhile . . .

"Mike, we had no idea that things were getting so serious so soon between you two," Dr. Lathan said.

"Yes, Dad, we've had these feelings for quite some time."

"You know, you could have or even should have talked to me about it, son."

"I know, Dad, you've always been available for me, but again, I didn't because I couldn't. What I mean is that I knew that I wanted to marry her the first time I laid eyes on her. My heart was overwhelmed by an apprehension from which there was no escape, yet the fear of her not feeling the same loomed in the back of my mind. And when our eyes met, it was a feeling my heart never knew. That moment, though just a moment, seemed like an eternal stare. I can't forget how my heart felt. I wish I could have taken a picture of what my heart saw so that I could share it with everyone, including her— no, especially her. Then she could see what a prisoner I've become to her."

"I never knew you were quite the Clark Gable type."

"Only the type that is stricken by her stare and paralyzed by her beauty."

"Dang it, boy, I'm really happy for both of you."

"Better let her know lunch is ready," Mrs. Lathan said as she entered the study.

"OK, Mom."

"Do you need me to take you to the airport in the morning?" Dr. Lathan asked.

"If you're not too tired."

"Too tired? What time does your flight leave?"

"At seven forty-five."

"Well, I'd better get my rest after dinner."

"Thanks, Dad!"

Later, after lunch, Mike and Rina spent some time together in the living room.

* * *

The next day, Mike and Rina's flight departed from Dallas, and they arrived at the Dulles International Airport. Misty was there to greet them. While driving to her home, Misty said, "Again, welcome, Mike! Rina, it's so grand to see you again, lady."

"You as well! It's great to be here in person."

"Mike, I'm just so happy to meet you. I must say, Rina, he is quite the looker. Better stay close to him."

"Easy there, girl. Slow your roll a bit, will you? He's quite responsible, so I trust his decision-making."

"It's not his decision-making you need to be concerned about. There are many single ladies in this town."

"Again, I believe I can trust him. He's romantic, not wild."

"OK, Rina!"

"So Misty, when do we meet your beau?"

"I'm sorry, guys. His name is Dean Connally, and he's in Japan for now. He's a naval commander stationed there for the next three years. But we communicate as often as we can, and he should be here for Christmas."

They arrived at Misty's house; a four-bedroom two-story. Mike carried their luggage into the living area.

"Will you two share the same bedroom or not?"

"That's a not! We love each other enough to save ourselves for our honeymoon," Rina said.

"That's so sweet! Old-fashioned, but sweet."

"Old-fashioned *and* sweet," Rina said.

"I've actually made arrangements to stay at the Hilton about twenty miles from here," Mike said.

"Nonsense, you two. Rina and I can take the two bedrooms in the east wing upstairs, and Mike, you can have the one in the west wing, or you can take the primary bedroom down here. It's your choice."

Mike made a quick call and canceled his hotel reservations.

"It would be nice to keep you out of trouble or, rather, keep trouble away from you, sweetheart. Just kidding around. He knows I like to kid, right, Mike?"

Mike smiled and changed the subject. "So, is Misty your given name, or is that short for something else?"

"Actually, my dad had to rush to the hospital from work during a misty fog and didn't know if he'd make it on time. All he could say was, 'It's so misty out there,' and that's all my mother could say when asked, 'What will you name her?'"

"That's so touching," Rina says.

"Wow, that's both cool and original. Anyway, Misty, how many will be taking part in this session on Monday?" Mike asked.

"So far, I have ten commitments, which includes you two and myself. Let's continue this in the dining room. I took the liberty of ordering pizza and Pepsi for lunch. I know you must be starved by now."

"Now is a great time for lunch, but afterward, you must show us your town," Mike said.

"OK then, let's save the pizza for a late-night snack. You remember those days, don't you, Rina?"

"Yes, oh too well. That's a habit I had a hard time breaking—and losing the extra pounds that it caused."

"I'm taking you two out for lunch on me to celebrate my girl's happiness and future. How does a prime rib sound, Mike?"

"Like music to my ears!"

They took a tour of the town, had lunch, and returned to Misty's home, settling into the living area to chat.

"Misty, what have you prepared to share with the group on Monday?" Mike asked.

"I started my research about a year ago when I read some articles in science journals from countries within the general areas surrounding the Ring of Fire. It was difficult at first, but I became obsessed with the work because I saw a pattern developing. But it's hard to determine if climate and temperature changes were a reason or a result of what was being detected. Myths began to surface, as well as scientific possibilities. Rina, has there been any weird activity around Mount Saint Helens lately?"

"Professor Dodds had me look into some mild trembling and some strange echoing, but we didn't find a reason for concern. Of course, you know the school doesn't have the equipment necessary to do what you can do here," Rina said.

"I was under the impression that you guys have a fantastic lab, more so than where I work. Remember, I was there for your birthday," Mike said.

"It's a very good lab, but I'm sure it can't compare to where you work, Misty," Rina said.

"Mike, let me get some files and notes I brought home. We'll take the rest of the week to go over them and prepare for the group session. Now, guys, let me be frank, OK? Some of this stuff is so far-fetched, it's crazy. But nothing can be left off the table. We must be true to our professions and our beliefs as well," Misty said.

"When you say 'our beliefs,' to what extent do you mean?" Mike questioned.

"To what extent? Actually, there are no boundaries, no fences, and no stop signs!"

They spread notes, graphs, and meter readings out over Misty's executive desk, arranging them in order based on time frames, and spent the remainder of the week brainstorming, reasoning, and analyzing the data as they finalized their presentations for the upcoming meeting, which was to begin the following Monday.

CHAPTER
FIFTEEN

Monday, July 16, 2046

I n the morning, they drove to the office of the Geological Survey Volcano Hazards Program in Reston where the holographic telepresence meeting was being held. The other scientists were from geological research offices from other parts of the globe. Misty beamed them in and started off the meeting.

"First of all, welcome to our first telepresence Ring of Fire meeting! Let me start by saying greetings to everyone.

"I would like to thank each of you for giving up your regular duties to share with us in this very uncertain time as we attempt to unravel the mystery of these unusual occurrences beneath the Earth's surface. Everyone who has collected data within the past four weeks, months, even within the last few years will be afforded the time and opportunity to share their findings and to give everyone their analysis. After each presentation, the floor will be opened for questions and discussion, then I will close out the presentation.

"We want to be sure that everyone present clearly understands the data and what it may signify so far as the Earth and human impact is concerned. That is, we want to be very clear of what your analysis is implying and how humanity and the Earth may be affected, whether in long- or short-term projections, even if concerns project far into our future, and how our descendants may be affected if that becomes a factor.

"So I will start by asking if you're ready. When your region is announced, will the representative for that team please bring up your region on the holographic projection and give us what you have. Remember, the floor will be open for questions, not refutations. We want to be sure everyone is taken seriously and understood clearly. This may take the better part of the first three or four days, given the schedule we'll be working with. Each day, we will have three two-hour sessions with two thirty-minute breaks and an hour lunch break. We'll start every day at eight thirty a.m. Eastern Standard Time and close at four thirty p.m. Eastern Standard Time."

Misty asked for the representative from the Australian office to present their findings. "Please begin."

"Let me start by saying greetings to everyone," he began. "Our research has been recorded over the past eighteen months. The areas that we've been monitoring expand from here, along the Indian-Australian Plate, to New Guinea through Norfolk Island to the Cocos Islands. Some of the activities we picked up were offshore to depths nearly reaching the Earth's core.

"Over the period that I mentioned, there's been what may appear to be cracking in the plate layers that seem to be a uniform pattern of zigzagging upward. At times, it even appeared that it might be a result of some type of openings being forced by pressure. Maybe lava, we thought at first, but there was no extreme heat detected. There was really no way that we could pinpoint an origin; it appeared that the origin was from everywhere.

"It seemed to just come upward from thousands of sources, like branches spreading from a tree's trunk, yet thousands of trunks. We considered whether anything could live at those depths under the ocean and actually be digging upward."

Hands went up.

The Australian representative pointed at a representative from Japan. "Yes, you have a question?"

"Sir, tell us, are you implying that our mythical Godzilla may not be a myth after all, and from beneath even the ocean's depth?"

"Sir, it's a direction that we considered, but I wouldn't in good faith call anything Godzilla," the Australian representative said. "But if there are creatures moving upward, it would be one heck of a discovery. Based on some of the unusually high, out-of-season waves, it could indicate shifting in the Earth's plates that may be sending shock waves upward and into the ocean. There have been a lot of high rivers and lakes causing strange flooding in strange places."

Another hand went into the air. A representative from the Philippines asked, "May I have an explanation of what is meant by 'strange flooding'?"

"Sir, one would expect flooding to occur in low-lying areas, but we've had flooding of rivers and lakes at the tops of mountain regions. We've had flooding when there was no rain to explain it. The water just seemed to ooze up out of the rocks of the mountains, which could be the result of plate shifts along underground lakes or underground oceans. So it could very well be water that's moving through the cracks and openings," the Australian representative replied.

* * *

Three days of similar presentations followed. On the fourth day, presentations were reaching an end with Misty's team, which included Mike and Rina. Rina's smartwatch vibrated, and she stepped out to answer the incoming message.

A few moments later, the first break came, and the meeting was paused. When Mike went outside, he saw a very teary-eyed Rina standing there, looking to be in shock. He rushed over to her.

"Rina! Rina, is everything OK?"

Rina began weeping bitterly and said, "No! No! Mike, I have to leave. Right now! I must get a flight home. My father's been killed in a bomb attack in a marketplace, and my mother's gravely wounded and is in the hospital. Amir just called. I'm so confused right now."

"Don't worry. I'm leaving with you."

"I appreciate that, but no, you have important work to do right here. I'll fly to Dallas, and Amir will meet me at the Love Field airport, and then we'll fly home from there."

Misty saw the concern in their expressions and rushed over. "Rina, are you ill or something?"

"She just got terrible news from her brother. Her father's been killed, and her mother is wounded," Mike said.

"Oh no! I'm so sorry, Rina!"

"I must get her to the airport. Can you make it alone until I return?"

"I'll get my secretary to postpone the rest of the day. We'll continue tomorrow."

"Misty, I'm so sorry. I know how important this is to you."

"Rina, don't even give it a second thought. Give me a couple of minutes to talk to my secretary, and then we'll go back to get your things. Mike, can you drive while I make Rina's flight arrangements?"

"Sure, I'll drive, but I feel that I must go with her."

"No, Mike," Rina said through her tears. "I know how much you care, but I also know how much Misty needs you for the rest of this session. You must present tomorrow. I'll call you later this evening, OK? Amir will meet me with tickets home. Don't worry, you two. I'll make it. I will."

"As soon as I get back to Dallas, I'll make flight plans to be with you, all right?"

"OK, sweetheart. I love you, Mike."

"I love you too."

Soon after, Rina got on her flight to Dallas Love Field Airport and met Amir there.

CHAPTER
SIXTEEN

The following day, the meeting continued, with Misty introducing the team from Ecuador.

"It is my pleasure to be invited to participate in this session, and I thank you, Dr. Myers, for your invite," the Ecuadorian representative said. "I would like to greet everyone present and hope that all render prayers for the young lady who had to leave due to a family emergency. I would like to start by showing you the region where our studies were conducted." He projected his region.

"We've been noticing for some months now, maybe eighteen to twenty, a rapidly increasing upward surge in what appears to be simply surface cracking. We have evidence to suggest that the westward movement of the South American Plate may be having more severe collisions with the Cocos Plate that is subducted beneath it, causing the cracking to be moving upward faster. There is something that is being detected on our seismometers that may be water, but it could also be natural gas. Some suggest that it could be oil that has seeped into the pattern of the openings. At one point some nine months ago, there were strange loud noises. One might suggest, but we could not determine, that those sounds echoing upward could be coming from something alive."

Several hands went up immediately.

"Yes, please. You, the Peruvian representative, you have a question?"

"Yes, I do, sir. Just how sure can you be that something could be alive down there where the plates meet? And how deep are you suggesting it could be?"

"Well, we can't be certain. It's just a theory based on specific patterns we picked up from the echoing, and these patterns do suggest some sort of communication. As far as the depth is concerned, again, there's no way of determining even an estimated depth. The strength of the sound waves varies tremendously, off and on. It's as though something moves through the cracking as far as it can and waits for another cracking to occur, then fills it until the end is reached. Over and over, we've made that deduction again throughout a period of months. But it could be some sort of fluid movement as well."

Members of the group asked the Ecuadorian representative a few more questions concerning the quaking and the frequency and strengths, which he went over.

The team from the United States then began their closing presentations. Misty called on the Yellowstone National Park representative.

"Greetings, ladies and gentlemen," the representative said. "I want to express what a privilege it is to be a part of this worldwide effort to attempt to unravel this mysterious scientific phenomenon." He pointed to the Yellowstone area on the holographic projection and continued. "This is our region of study, extending from the Long Valley Caldera through the Bishop ash bed, bending around Huckleberry Ridge ash bed through the Texas Panhandle semicircle through northern Oklahoma, Kansas, and most of Colorado. I want to thank

Dr. Myers of the Virginia office, our team leader who also teamed us with the Mount Saint Helens office.

"I'd like to say that I wonder if the animals of Yellowstone know something that we don't. For about three years now, they've seemed to be quite agitated about small quaking and roaring coming from seismic activity that never seemed to bother them before, even to the point of acting as though something is scaring them. Animals have strategically been trying to escape the park, walking the boundary lines, and constantly challenging the integrity of the fences and the intensity of the electric line barriers.

"Something for sure has them spooked. It's getting more difficult to contain them, as well as to find methods of calming them. We don't know if there is something besides lava that is beneath the surface or how deep it might be. Our seismometers have been unstable with what we're picking up, making it almost impossible to nail down a true cause. We do know that what is going on has our animals on high alert, but for what?

"There is such a wide area of concern covering the entire western half of the United States. Our readings seem to be coming from at least thirteen states within the south central and northwestern quadrant. We're totally baffled as to the true source of these disturbances in our readings. I've had the opportunity to spend some time with one of our US colleagues in the past couple of days who I believe has a very interesting theory, so I'd like to yield the floor to Dr. Michael T. Lathan Jr. Please come up to the front, Dr. Lathan."

Mike came forth.

"I would like to, if I may, welcome all of you to this meeting, and I thank Dr. Myers for her invite and the confidence she has in me. Most of my research has been done in seismic activity around the Dallas, Arlington, and Irving, Texas, areas. There's been a lot of quaking in the past four years, much of which can be attributed to fracking. Most of the quaking has been minor, not exceeding 2.5 to 3.3 on the Richter scale. Until lately, it has not caused much concern.

But recently, even small quakes in one area have been felt two or three states away, leading us to believe that this has gone beyond fault lines and plate subducting.

"I would like to piggyback on something our Peruvian colleague mentioned with a theory I'd like to present. I know that it may seem far-fetched to most of you, but there seems to be some truth to what he proposed. Dr. Myers, Professor Adelstein, and I did some comparisons on the data coming from three of our offices in different locations: Yellowstone, Mount Saint Helens, and the Texas-Oklahoma regions."

Mike brought up a graph.

"Please don't focus on the complexity of the graph, but instead, look at intelligence that is implicated in the patterning. There seems to be a pattern of time from this zigging move to this point, which stopped for at least seven months and then started again for about the same time, covering the same distance."

A hand went up.

"Yes, sir, you have the floor."

"I'm from a region near the Aleutian Trench in Anchorage, Alaska. Dr. Lathan, you say there's time duration in the movement and a systematic manner of movement, so just what are you implying? Are you really saying that you believe intelligent beings are causing the quaking, the roaring, and if so, what proof do you have to back up such a claim?"

"Is anybody in here smarter than a fifth grader?" He chuckled. "Hmm, OK. When I was a fifth grader, I had to do a science project, and what interested me most was ants. My father helped me put together an ant farm. I was totally fascinated, and I fell in love with the intelligence of the colony. What struck me as we put this graph together was what it resembled. I was reminded of my fifth-grade project because my father and I had put a glass pane over a shallow box about two inches deep, three feet tall, and about four and a half feet long with some ants and their queen. It was amazing to me as a fifth grader to see the pattern in which the ants traveled to the surface to get food. They burrowed tunnels we called runners to their bedding area, which resembled a cave with several levels and entrances.

"As I compared our graphs with that ant farm in my mind, I was shocked, amazed, and at the same time dumbfounded. To even consider that to be possible, one might consider ants up to maybe three to six inches long all over the world working to get to the surface."

A roar of conversation filled the room, loud and constant. Misty had to ask for order. "Are there any more questions?" she asked after the uproar had quieted. "Dr. Lathan, I'll turn things back over to you."

"The representative from Alaska, I see you have another question," Mike said.

"Actually, I have a two-part question. The first part is related to an observation, and what I would like to know is, are you related to Rev. Dr. Michael Lathan, the famous preacher?"

"Yes, he's my father," Mike said.

"I remember seeing you on one of his programs, teaching a series on end-time events. There was one lesson in particular that interested me—"

Mike, quickly interrupting, said, "I want to be careful not to turn this meeting into a continuation on that series, sir, but we can discuss it at another time. So what is the second part of your question?"

"Are these worldwide events that have taken place over the past few years ushering in the end of time as we know it, and if so, how much time do we have, based on your findings?"

"Hold on, now. Not to my knowledge, and that was a three-part question."

"Seriously, Dr. Lathan, just what is your final finding implying? To your knowledge."

"Actually, we've not reached a final finding. We're still exploring data and others' ideas as well."

"So who will determine what the final findings will be, and when will that decision be made?"

"We were looking for input here this week to give us more to work with because, obviously, there will be more meetings like this one in the near future. But for now, we're going to consider everything that has been shared here this week by all the speakers, do more analysis of the inputs, and work from there."

Misty came forth.

"At this point, I would like to thank every one of you for sharing your findings. Again, as Dr. Lathan stated, this is only a preliminary gathering. I'm going to set up other sessions with other locations' representatives after sharing what we've received this week with my boss and his staff. Some of you will be invited to come again to help us move further along in the process of reaching conclusions that we feel everyone will be comfortable with. Look for my calls or emails. It's time to close this session, and my team has enjoyed everyone's input. Be safe, be careful, and goodbye. It is four-thirty, and this session is now closed."

After the others had left, Misty asked, "Mike, can you please help me gather these materials to take home?"

"Sure thing, Misty. Afterward, can you take me back to that steak house? What was the name of it?"

"Sure, it's called the Angus Restaurant. I'll buy."

"I'm starved. Let's go!"

"Tell me, how long have you considered your theory concerning the creatures that you believe are moving upward toward the Earth's crust? And what timeline have you come up with?" Misty asked as they left the conference room.

"Actually, I began to put together the facts concerning events that started happening in 2038—the burning hail all over the world, the very peculiar oceanic phenomenon with the gigantic underwater vortex a few years later, and the strange viruses that attacked the world's water supplies and killed so many people were enough to cause me to do some serious Bible research, as well as scientific. What I was seeing prompted me to discuss with my father, a Bible scholar, the possibility of some sort of tie-in. Of course, he's all Bible and revelations in respect to what's been going on with the weather."

"Well, what is his take?"

"He cautioned me to be very sure of what I proposed and be very, very clear. He said that when you're dealing with tight-knit groups, you can put a lot of information on the table. But when you're considering what you can put to the public in comparison to what you should, you must be wise. With something so widespread, people need to know what's going on, but in order to honor protocol, one must consult with the US government and present the factual findings to them, then let them decide what the public should hear.

"He further warned me of publicly pointing toward the end of time. That's been a problem for decades. Many have attempted to sway the public for their own personal gains of fame, prestige, and of course, money. But you know, Misty, Rina and I have discussed that point on several occasions. She's more scientific in her perspective and considers many possibilities. I've shared with her the prophecy of the events leading up to the ushering in of the end of days. The frightful thing is that I'm convinced that we're the generation that will experience it."

"Please explain to me, if you would, what it is about the events that have taken place that has you so convinced? You know that people all over the world will have various thoughts about your mental conditioning."

"Yes, you're right. They'll think that I'm a religious nutcase. But that's not what scares me."

"Just what does scare you, then?"

"What might happen next!"

"Should I be afraid to ask?"

"Very, but I really hope I'm wrong."

CHAPTER
SEVENTEEN

Mike took a flight home early the following morning and had breakfast with his father. As they ate, Dr. Lathan asked him, "Well, son, how'd your presentation go?"

"The presentation went as I expected," Mike responded. "Some may be thinking that I was a bit overly religious, and that was expected as well. But Rina had to leave early. Her father was killed in a bombing at a marketplace, and her mother's in very bad condition."

Mrs. Lathan asked him as she took a seat at the table, "Did I hear you correctly? Rina's dad was killed, and her mother was wounded?"

"Unfortunately, yes, Mom," Mike said. "I don't know what to do. I can't find words to comfort her."

"When you speak with her and Amir, please extend our condolences to their family, and please let Rina know not to hesitate if there's anything we can do. They're such a sweet family, and we want them to know we are here for them. I hope her mother is going to be all right."

"Thank you, Mom. I'll let her know as soon as I speak to her. I haven't had a chance to catch up with her yet. I'm sure she and her family are hurting and are busy with trying to sort out things and prepare for her father's memorial service."

"This is such a tragedy. Give her a couple of days to sort matters out and then give her a call," his mother responded.

Mike, looking sad and feeling helpless, said, "I'm sure you're right, but I want to speak to her so badly."

"I know how you must feel," Dr. Lathan said, "but your mother's right, son. She's going to need that time with her family."

"I know she wants to talk to me as well, but . . ."

"Mike, just give her a couple of days to be with her family, then call and check on her."

"Perhaps . . ."

* * *

The next day, Mike called Rina, and she told him she was with Amir and other family members planning her father's memorial service. She told him that her mother's injuries were critical, and she was still in the hospital.

Mike expressed his feelings of wanting to fly to Tel Aviv to be with her during this difficult time. Rina warmly appreciated his thoughtfulness and concern to be with her; however, she suggested that he should wait a few weeks because she and Amir really needed to spend some time with their mother. They also needed to take care of some other matters because their father had always handled the family's business affairs.

Mike was a little apprehensive. However, he said he understood and would call her back in a few days to check on her.

Some days later, Mike called Rina, and she informed him that she was going to have to stay there with her mother at least until she got out of the hospital and her condition improved. Furthermore, Amir would be flying back to Dallas in a couple of weeks, and it was imperative that one of them stayed there with their mother.

Rina also told Mike that she had spoken to Professor Dodds and Misty and told them it would probably be a few months before she could come back to America. Mike was concerned about her job, and she let him know that everything was all right. Professor Dodds was arranging for her to take a family leave. She assured Mike that everything was going to be all right, but of course, he was still concerned.

"OK, this is good to hear," Mike said. "I will let you concentrate on your mom and your family affairs and will get back to you in a couple of days, but you call me if you need me or just want to talk. I don't care what time it is. Promise me you'll call me. I'm here for you. I love you."

"OK, I will. I love you too, and I miss you. I'll say good night now."

"Rina, my parents and I extend our condolences for the loss of your father, and we're praying for your mother to recover."

"Thank you so much. I love you so much. Talk to you soon."

* * *

Two days later, Mike called to check on Rina.

"Hi, Mike!"

"Hi, Rina! How are you, and how is your mother?"

"I'm doing OK, considering the circumstances, but Mom is still in the hospital, and we're taking it a day at a time. She's resting very comfortably, though."

"Good, I'm glad to hear that. Do you need anything? Can I send you anything? Do you need me to call anyone?"

"No, I don't need anything. I'm fine. Professor Dodds has gotten approval for me to take some family leave time, so that's good. It's giving me time to take care of things here at home and spend more time with Mother. Misty called and checked on me. She is really concerned about me, but we have been communicating through video calls, and it makes her feel better to be able to see me."

"That's great! I miss you so much, and I'm praying every day for God to help you through this. I'm just a phone call away."

They continued their conversation for about an hour before Rina said she was ready for bed. They had set one up in her mother's room for Rina to sleep nearby.

Rina ended up staying in Tel Aviv longer than she had planned, for several months, but she and Mike stayed in contact and talked almost every day.

CHAPTER
EIGHTEEN

Mike got a text from Rina: *Need to talk to you so badly! Mom's not doing too well, I'm afraid. Call me please!*

Mike immediately made a video call to Rina.

"Hello, Mike, darling. I've just learned that my mother might not make it. The doctors say she has gotten worse and has less than a fifteen percent chance of surviving. Over half her body suffered shrapnel damage, some of which, if removed, will kill her."

"I'm on my way, babe. Hold on till I get there, OK?"

"I need to see you as soon as possible."

"I've been trying to make flight plans, but your country is still under a public transportation high-security alert. But Dad said I could use his jet and his pilots, so I just have to clear it through customs and see how I can handle it. I'll call you as soon as I get it worked out."

"Yes, maybe Amir can fly with you. We miss him and need him here."

"That's fine. I'll contact him. I'll see you when I get there. I'll call you to let you know where we'll be."

"Amir can help you plan that."

"Stay strong, honey. I'll see you in a few days. Bye-bye."
"I'll be waiting for your arrival. Goodbye! Love you!"

* * *

Three days later, Mike received a call from Rina.

"Hello, Rina, what's going on? Is everything OK?"

"No, Mike, everything's wrong. I spent the morning with Mother, and she seemed stable. I went to breakfast, but when I returned, she had passed on. I've already contacted Amir and told him."

"Oh my, I don't know what to say. I'm so sorry, Rina, my darling. Last evening, I got everything squared away for a flight; however, I'll see if we can get it moved up. I'll call you when we arrive. I was able to get a commercial flight, so we'll fly back to Dallas, get Dad's jet, and then I'll take you back to Washington."

"All right. When you two get here, Amir can help me with the funeral arrangements. I'll be waiting. Goodbye, love."

"OK, babe, see you when we get there."

* * *

When Mike and Amir arrived at the airport in Tel Aviv, Rina was waiting.

They greeted one another with hugs, and Mike said, "Rina, I'm so sorry about your mother, but I'm here for you both. You look spent. When is the last time you had something to eat?"

"I don't know," Rina replied. "I just haven't thought about it."

"We understand, Sister, but you look as though you need something now," Amir said.

"Let's find an eatery," Mike said.

"There's a nice deli by gate fifteen. It's not far," Amir said.

"Not far? We're at gate one," Rina said.

"We have time. I'll get you one of those riding carts I saw earlier."

"No, I'll be OK. Let's get something. I'm hungry."

The funeral was held a week later, and then they prepared to fly back to Dallas.

Good Friday, April 12, 2047

Amir, Mike, and Rina arrived back in Dallas, Texas and Amir went home, however, Mike and Rina went to Mike's parents' home.

Mike and Rina were set to fly to Washington, so they decided to have breakfast at the Lathans' house before taking their flight. During the meal, they discussed their schedule for the next couple of days.

Mrs. Lathan, looking out of the glass door leading to the pool patio, said, "Honey, have you looked outside? It doesn't appear that the sun has risen yet. How strange."

Suddenly, the entire house began to shake violently for about three seconds, then stopped. A loud growling sound could be heard.

"Oh my!" Mrs. Lathan yelled. "Did any of you feel that?"

"Feel that? We saw and heard that!" Mike said.

Dr. Lathan, looking concerned, said, "I was in LA preaching at a convention when that horrible earthquake happened, and strangely enough, it felt and sounded the same."

"An earthquake in Texas? How could that be?" Mrs. Lathan asked.

"There is a fault line stretching through Texas. And a scientific report published in 2011 noted giant cracks forming in the Earth all over the globe. The scientific world is baffled. Yet the Bible's prophecies predicted worldwide earthquakes," Mike said.

Mrs. Lathan, looking outside again, said, "Hello! Does anyone besides me see how dark it is out there?"

"It's still morning, dear. What do you expect, a sun blast?" replied Dr. Lathan.

Mrs. Lathan, still peering through the patio door, said, "It's after eight, and I can't see anything but darkness!"

Rina looked out the window. "Wow! I see what you mean, ma'am. It's totally dark."

Mike now approached and stood next to Rina. "One might call it pitch dark. How strange! Wonder what it could mean?"

Mrs. Lathan turned on the monitor in the room and flipped through the channels to the world news stations. "Maybe we'll get some answers," she said.

Total darkness was being reported from all over the world. It was around 2:00 p.m. in London, and there was no sun, not even a hint of brightness. It was 9:00 p.m. in China, and there were hardly any stars giving light. The moon had been shining brightly and then just disappeared.

"How strange! And there are reports of accidents of all kinds. What a tragedy! What in the world is going on?" Mrs. Lathan said.

"Oh my God!" Mike said.

"Careful, Dr. Scientist. You're in danger of sounding like a Bible-toting preacher," Dr. Lathan said to Mike.

Mrs. Lathan drew their attention back to the news. "Look, QUIK News is airing reports coming from the US Naval Observatory. They're saying that the sun appears to be in its proper orbit and looks to be fully intact, but it's not glowing normally. The far side of the sun seems to have some glow, but it's dull and flickering!"

"Mike, could it be that your theory may have serious merit?" Dr. Lathan asked.

"Well, Father, we discussed many possible facets of that theory, so which one are you referring to?"

"Oh, come on, Mike, look outdoors and see what's happening!"

"Remember the warnings you gave me about what should and what shouldn't be released to the public?"

"Son, the public is being introduced to something beyond our understanding."

"Hold on, guys, listen to these reports," Mrs. Lathan said.

Reports came from the Griffith Observatory and the international space weather agencies. They said that they had considered that some stars might have just changed position, taking their bit of light with them, but closer observations revealed that the stars were still in their orbits, but their light had just gone out. They also reported that the moon showed evidence of about thirty percent of its mass being blacked out.

"Well, Dr. Scientist and Dr. Divinity, what have you to say? Are there answers for this?" asked Mrs. Lathan.

"Mom, I'm sure we'll find out. Rina, it looks like we're going to have to ride this one out before I can get you home. Is that OK?" responded Mike.

"I've been away from home for months now anyway. I guess there's no estimated time, huh?"

"I would like to say just a few hours, but if I'm correct, there may be questions I'm not ready to answer. Besides, Professor Dodds told you to take as much time as you need. I think maybe you should spend more time here."

"Well, Amir said he and his family would love to have an in-house sitter for as long as I need to stay. Besides, it would be nice to be around family awhile longer."

"I'm sure there's a lot of worldwide panic—people who were taking their children to schools, people trying to get to work. Many outside workers are probably being told not to go to their job sites because of the associated dangers and so much traffic," Mike said.

"That's definitely true," Mrs. Lathan said. "Here on this station, they said a construction worker was seriously injured and another one killed in Fort Worth, Texas, when a backhoe someone tried to operate by streetlight fell into the trench it was digging, pulling one worker in and then crushing him. Everything's so dangerous right now. School buses have been grounded. They are warning everyone to just stay home. It's a wonder that there are no reports of crime outbreaks. I guess even the criminals are too cautious to go out right now."

* * *

People all around the world experienced total darkness for over eight hours before daylight, stars, and the moon began to shine again. Life continued but with much confusion. The top scientists were baffled as well.

It was now a little after 4:00 p.m., and Rina and Mike were still at the Lathans' home.

"Oh my, look, everyone, daylight is restored! Mike, I guess you can take me to Amir's house now," Rina said.

"Why don't you have dinner and rest for the remainder of the day, Rina?" Mike asked.

"I'd like nothing better than to go back to work at the lab, but it makes sense that I get some rest. The last few months have been very hard on me."

"Yes, I'm sure of that. Don't forget that we've got a lot to discuss as well. It'll be nice having you so close to me."

"I know and we shall."

"This year, I want to spend New Year's Eve there with you. I love that part of the country during that season."

"Are you saying that you will spend Christmas at home with us?" Mrs. Lathan asked.

"I'm old and tired. I was hoping to have you help me with services on Christmas Day," Dr. Lathan added.

"Yes, that's correct. I'll be here for Christmas, but I must spend New Year's Eve with my fiancée, OK?"

"It's a deal. Right, honey?" asked Mrs. Lathan.

"Yes, it's a deal," Dr. Lathan agreed.

* * *

Later that evening, Mike prepared to take Rina to Amir's home.

"Mom, Dad, you do remember that—"

"Yes, we do remember. You're headed to Seattle on New Year's Eve," Dr. Lathan said.

"Yes, we do, Mike," Mrs. Lathan added. "I hate to break the tradition of all of us being together as a family and asking God's blessing for the New Year. But we did agree, and we understand."

"Son," Dr. Lathan said. "Be careful and keep your eyes open. I'm sure you're aware of all the volcanic activity that's been reported lately, especially around Mount Saint Helens."

"Yes, I am. As a matter of fact, I've talked to Rina and Dr. Myers about it. Dr. Myers has been in communication with some of the offices that attended the session in Reston in July, and our data indicate that the activities we discussed are much closer to the Earth's surface lately."

"What does it mean?" Dr. Lathan asked.

"I have my suspicions, but the other scientists' suspicions differ quite a bit, so we'll see. We will see."

Mike then took Rina to Amir's home.

CHAPTER
NINETEEN

November 2047

Some nine years after the fiery hailstorm, Beatrice Bolden, Tim's wife, was in the bathroom getting ready for work. Looking in the mirror while brushing her teeth after a good, hot shower, she noticed smudgy markings on her forehead. At first, she considered that she hadn't removed all her makeup the night before. She grabbed a dry face towel and gave it a few rubs, but when that didn't work, she got some makeup remover and swabbed the marks for a few seconds, to no avail.

"Tim! Tim! Are you awake yet?" she called out.

"Uhhh, barely, Bea. What do you need?"

"I need you to come to the bathroom for a minute."

"Bea, as much as I'd like to, we don't have time to play."

"Don't flatter yourself, fella. I don't want to have to shower again anyway. I want you to see something."

Still flirting while on his way to the bathroom, he said, "What is it that I haven't seen before?"

"Knock it off and get in here, will you?"

As Tim walked through the bathroom door, he said, "Let's see what you've got for me, sexy mama."

"Where is that enthusiasm when I desire it? Look at my forehead and tell me what you see."

"Well, let's see . . . first, about two feet of forehead."

"Get serious now and look closer! Tell me if you see letters or something like it."

"Wow! Yes, I see. But if these are letters, they were made by a drunk chicken. Who's the drunken rooster that's writing on your forehead, woman?"

"Tim, one of these days, I'm gonna leave you, fool!"

"Where you gonna go? Home to your mama?

"Don't make me fire you right now, knuckle head!"

"You sound like a corporate boss now."

"I think I may have to take off work and go to my doctor's office and get this checked out."

"You gonna get paid? You know you don't get paid if you take off work the day after Thanksgiving! Wait till Monday evening."

"Well, I'll see if I can get an appointment for this evening after work. Her last appointment is at five thirty. I hope this isn't something I caught at work or church," she said.

"Been in any chicken coops lately?"

"If I didn't love you, I'd kill you right now, you mentally challenged fool! I'll call my doctor when I get to work. If I get an appointment, I'll call you to let you know."

"Have you tried chicken-scratch remover? Just teasing, darling. Talk to you later, OK?"

"I'm not coming home after I leave the doctor's office—actually, ever again!"

"Love you too, sweetheart! Talk to you if you—I'm sorry—when you come back."

* * *

Beatrice arrived at work and greeted a church member coworker, Shirley.

"Beatrice, what's that on your forehead?" Shirley asked.

"I'm not sure, but it's scaring me."

"Yeah, me too!"

"You too?"

"Yes, meet me in the ladies' room, and I'll show you what I mean."

In the restroom, Shirley brushed back her bangs with her fingers. Her markings were quite light, hardly noticeable, whereas Beatrice's were very heavy but not clearly defined.

"See, it's not as heavy as yours, but I got scared too. My husband, the biblical scholar, teasingly said, 'It's started. God is marking His sheep before the slaughter.'"

"I know what you mean. I promised to kill Tim if I go back home this evening. He was teasing me so much."

"What do you think? Think there might be something to what my husband said?"

"Girl, it's 2047, nowhere near the end of time! According to our pastor, a lot of other things must take place first," Beatrice said.

"Well, you know a lot of strange things have taken place within the last nine years. Things that have been mentioned in the book of Revelation."

"Yeah, we were enjoying a backyard barbecue when the hail-storm of 2038 happened," Beatrice said. "That was bizarre indeed, and all that other crazy stuff that happened all over the world. But the start of the end-time? I don't know."

"You won't hear that coming from my lips. I'm not ready to be called a nutcase by the public," Shirley responded.

"We know it's gonna start sometime, maybe soon. Who knows for sure?"

"Right, who can be sure? Heck, people have been predicting the end of time for ages, as far as I know. Ain't happened yet!"

"But it will happen! When? I won't be the one to try to nail down a date or a time."

* * *

That evening after Beatrice got off work, she went to her doctor's appointment. "Hello, Dr. Gupta," she said.

"Hello, Beatrice, what seems to be bothering you so?" Dr. Gupta asked.

"Look at my forehead."

"I'll be frank with you: As strange as it is, I've seen quite a number of these cases in the past few days. In all the ones I've seen and done skin and blood tests on, the results are the same. No signs of any infections, no skin diseases, and no chemicals such as ink, dye, or paints are present."

"So what do you think it could be?"

"Well, I don't know what to think, so I can't say! I only know that the markings differ, and the tones and shades vary from very light to very dark. I can say that I don't believe it's a health risk; rather, it's a sign or signet of some sort."

"Of what? And why me?"

"Maybe it's something spiritual. Heck, I don't know. I do know it's very unusual."

"Funny thing, Doctor, my husband—that heathen—he doesn't have it. Why does this sort of thing always happen to saved folk?"

"Maybe it's your test. We already know where the heathens are going."

"Don't we know it. I tell Tim all the time, he'd better get saved."

"Well, I wish I had more I could tell you. But maybe it's from getting older. So don't worry. It's not dangerous. See you next time," Dr. Gupta said.

* * *

Beatrice returned home at about 6:30 p.m. and was greeted with more strange news from Tim.

"Hey, honey, what did the doctor say? Anything useful?"

"She doesn't think it's dangerous and says she's seen several cases in the last few days. Told me not to worry."

"Strange enough, I've received several calls today from Torey, Billy, Courtney, and Andy, all saying that either their wives and/or they themselves have developed some markings on their foreheads in the past week or so. I told them that you thought the end of time might be near. Andy said it better not be. Heck, he said he just got clean and ain't had time to get saved. But he promised to do so as soon as Sunday comes."

"Hope he has time. As a matter of fact, you'd better get saved yourself, heathen!"

"You truly are the diva of doom, as my folks say!"

"Tell them they're supposed to love the message, not hate the messenger!"

"Let's turn on the news and see if this is a common occurrence in other places."

As they flipped through the news channels, they saw similar cases being discussed all over the world.

"Even some of the commentators and clergies have similar markings," Beatrice said. "I wonder if they're worried. They didn't appear to be. I told you that God was tired of you and your heathen brothers and everybody like them. Whether you all want to admit it or not, you can see that I was right! Now, either you confess your sins and renounce evil, or you will regret the day you were born."

"You know, I hadn't said anything, but I've been thinking about going to church with you soon," Tim says.

"How soon might that be?"

"When is the next time it'll be open?"

"The next time it'll be open? You're joking, right? The church doesn't open. We have service on different days. What made you want to change? You're scared now, aren't you?"

"Scared? No, honey, I've just become aware that I'm not in control of my own life, and you don't control it either!"

"See, you're not really concerned. You're scared! Whatever it takes, I guess God can use that too!"

"Seriously, my brothers and I have discussed it a lot over the past few years. We believe it's about time we give our lives over to God."

"We? Y'all? All? Hallelujah! Hallelujah! He's still working miracles! Now let me be serious again. I was quite serious years ago, but you couldn't see it. You and your heathen folks were too far gone."

"OK, sweetheart, enough with the insults. We're all serious now. Let's work with that fact."

"That's great, hon. I'm happy for all of you. Don't change your minds. He won't like it!"

"When are you going to pray for Him to remove that scribble from your forehead? Ha!"

"Really? I'm gonna pray that you and your folks all get one. If you knew what I know, you'd thank me for that prayer!"

* * *

At about 8:00 p.m., Janie, who lived in Australia, contacted Kaye—her elder sister who had the gift of dreams and visions—via a holographic call.

"Hello, Janie, what's been going on with you? I haven't talked to you in quite some time. And how's that unsaved mate of yours?" Kaye asked with a laugh.

"Please stop it. That unsaved mate you're speaking of is, in fact, my husband, you know."

"The Bible says that saved people should be equally yoked, not choked by the weight of sin hanging around our necks."

"Stop it! That's enough, now! I love him despite his short-comings."

"If you love him, get him saved. Speaking seriously, though, what's going on with you?"

"Well, first of all, tell me what you think about all the weird things that have been going on since 2038 and how they might relate to religion, if at all?"

"Well, about forty-five days before the hailstorm in 2038, I had a series of visions and dreams. I even had an out-of-body experience."

"Really? Well, what's really going on?"

"For about a week, every night while lying in bed, I would go into a trancelike state, and I would see boats being pulled to the bottom of the oceans. I saw people being poisoned and others losing control of their minds and some dying. One night, I saw myself standing in my yard. It was real. I was there! Watching grass and trees burning all around our houses. I tell you, it was so real, and it was frightening."

"What did you think it meant, Kaye?"

"I didn't get any interpretation because it was not clear to me at all. It was as though the world was about to end. I was relieved to snap out of it. But I was left with much concern until the events actually happened."

"How does it tie into the future?"

"I'm not certain, but there are Scriptures in Revelation that may be similar, and they do, in fact, point toward the end of time on Earth."

"If there's a connection, it's time for a worldwide revival. But how do we convince the world?"

"We don't. But the events, if they continue, will. So why did you really call me?"

"Well, when I was getting ready for work the other morning, I noticed some strange markings on my forehead that have me quite concerned. My doctor says it's not something dangerous, though, because there's no sign of toxins or poisons. No chemicals present either."

While wiping her hair from her forehead, Kaye asked, "Does it look anything like this?" Kaye had markings that resembled a glowing foreign type of scribble.

"Yes, like that, yet different," Janie said, removing her scarf from her head and pointing to her mark. "So what do you think it means?"

"I know what I hope it means, but do I really hope for it or not?"

"All right now, Kaye, have you gotten into the sacrament wine?"

"If it's what I hope it is, it is the mark of God before the great hurt of Abaddon/Apollyon, which is the last event of the first woe."

"Can we convince the world of that fact?"

"It won't be easy. The world will deem us insane! But all the facts are not in place yet."

"What's missing?"

"You might not want to know!"

CHAPTER
TWENTY

Thanksgiving and Christmas Holiday Season—2047

Rina ended up staying in Dallas with Amir and his family for a few months and decided to spend Thanksgiving with Mike and his parents.

"Rina, I understand you are now quite the accomplished scientist," Dr. Lathan said.

"Thank you, sir. I do enjoy both teaching and also the research I do at the university."

"Aww, you're being modest," Mike said. "She is quite the researcher in the field, and she has discovered a lot of new things, though her main research field of study has been atmospheric change —you know, the movement of stars, meteors, and advancing climate change. She was at her best during the strange hailstorm of 2038, as I was told by her mentor, Professor Dodds."

"Yes, but we came away from that with little, if anything."

"But you gained valuable experience during that period," Mike said.

"OK, enough with the blind accolades," Rina said.

"Rina, tell me your thoughts on Mike's theory about the cracks—or tunnels, if you will—that have formed beneath the Earth's crust," Mrs. Lathan said.

"While at Dr. Myers's home, we compared data findings. Not to say that I'm on Mike's spiritual level, but I can say that I do believe that there is more than nature at work here."

"Elaborate if you dare," Dr. Lathan said.

"Well, we know that there are many forms of life beneath the Earth's crust, but until the last few years, we'd never observed a systematic ascent toward the surface. It's almost like they're moving in a seasonal trend."

"Hmm. Are you saying that you believe there could be intelligence at work?"

"It is the only thing that makes good sense, whether scientific, natural, or spiritual," Rina said. "Whichever of these it may be, no one will know until whatever they are make it through the surface."

"OK, Dr. Mike, what do you say about your own theory?" Dr. Lathan asked.

"I can only hope that Mother Nature is playing a dirty trick on our instruments, if that doesn't sound too earthly. Because if that's not the case, we could be experiencing the fulfillment of prophecy, which would be my number one evaluation."

Mrs. Lathan raised her eyebrow. "Then what would be your number two?"

"Again, Mother Nature's dirty trick. But considering all the strange weather phenomena and life-taking events, what I believe is that this is the generation that will experience things or events—some I believe may have already taken place—that will usher in the end-time."

"Do you know how you sound or what you are saying?" Dr. Lathan asked. "Your theory doesn't imply but directly states a theological explanation. Be careful. That's all I'm saying."

"Dad, you're a Bible scholar. What do you think based on recent events, including the total darkness that happened months ago and lasted for eight or more hours? Come on, don't be passive. Let's hear from you, Dad!"

"Whatever's going on should be left to the scientists, son."

"Dad, that's who we are. Rina, Dr. Myers, Professor Dodds, and myself, we're scientists. But I'm also a Bible scholar, or have you forgotten? I believe in what the Bible says, what prophecy says."

"Tell us, Mike, what does prophecy say? And why does prophecy say it?"

"Dad, are you really going there with me after all our discussions? Have you changed? What are you afraid of? You, of all people! But if you must go there, let me lay a crystal foundation. In Matthews 24, the Bible clearly expresses that the generation who witnesses a series of certain catastrophic events will be the generation who will experience the ushering in of the end times. I believe we are that generation that has begun to see the ushering in of the end-time events. Again, I further believe that the catastrophes spoken of started some nine or ten years ago."

"Whoa, son, that theory will bring a lot of skepticism, wouldn't you say? Even some scorn from church leaders."

"Surely, but it won't change the outcome! Now, back to the latest data collected from around the world. For some strange reason, the cracking has taken on a change in direction. It appears that the cracking seems to be moving toward all the major volcanoes, including Mount Saint Helens and Yellowstone National Park. If you will remember, a few years ago is when most of the wild animals in the park were trying to escape and seemed very skittish. Maybe they were warning us."

"Maybe? If it is truly prophecy, they were warning us. But come on, Mike, do you really think you can sell that theory?"

"Well, what is selling if not convincing? Warning *is* a good sell. There is so much wrong with human interactions that a warning can give us time to get it right."

"Exactly what do you propose to be the main human flaw?"

"I believe that the continued disregard of spiritual, moral, ethical, and humane principles has afforded to man a predicted outcome, which is now being played out, to our detriment. I believe it's going to get worse."

"All prophecy must be fulfilled, right?"

"I further believe that each of us controls our own position and how our lives can and will be affected!"

"Now you're speaking of changing the hearts of all humankind. Do you really believe that's possible?"

"That's what our job as proclaimers is all about. I believe the reward is worth the risk."

"You remind me of just how brilliant you really are. I'm so proud. So what's your agency's next move?"

"Rina and I need to meet with Dr. Myers and some of our colleagues in the science world to determine what that might be. Mom, thank you for yet another great dinner. I'm going to take Rina to Amir's now, and I'll talk with you next week, OK? See you all later. Rina, I'll help you get your things, and then we'll head out."

* * *

Mike called Rina on Christmas Day.

"Hello, sweetheart, how are things there at Amir's?"

"Things are great. I miss you, though. I haven't seen or talked to you in a week."

"Yes, well, Father had me doing quite a bit of his running around since he claims to be so old and so tired. But it needs to be done, and I do enjoy being so connected to my family. Speaking of such, I know I agreed to allow you this time with your family, and I'm committed to mine, but I think a window will open that I can jump out of and bring you your Christmas gift."

"A window? Won't that be dangerous? Your parents' windows are quite high. I'd love to see you, though."

"Not a *window* window but a window in time. My aunt and uncle will be dropping by in a few. That'll keep my parents occupied for a couple of hours. An opportunity for us, OK?"

"Of course, and you know I was just teasing. I know what you meant! Call me when you're on the way so that I can be ready. We can use the porch hammock."

"Sounds romantic. Wow!"

"Call me and stop it!"

* * *

Two hours later, Rina received a video call from Mike, then he showed up fifteen minutes later. While they sat on the hammock, he said, "Rina, I don't want you to go back to Washington. I know what you've gone through, and I want to be available for you. I want you to stay."

"This is sudden!"

"Well, babe, I've been monitoring seismic activity around the Washington region, and it's getting more unpredictable by the minute. Record numbers of quakes per day. It's not much better in Oregon, Idaho, Montana, or Wyoming—even as far north as Edmonton, Canada—and heck, I'm too concerned."

"You know, Mike, I'm really concerned too."

"I've been thinking . . . Let's just make plans to get married," he suggested.

"I'm ready to marry you. Let's pick a date."

"All right, it's settled. How about April first?"

"Michael! That's not happening! That's April Fools' Day! Is that your contingent escape plan for later years?"

"Babe, you know I was just kidding. So how's June?"

"Well, we'd discussed May or June before things got so strange, but I think I like June . . . the sixth. How's that for you?"

"June sixth it is."

Mike pulled out a beautifully wrapped Christmas gift and handed it to her. "Here's your present!"

"Oh Mike!" Rina opened the gift and saw a beautiful set of diamond earrings with a diamond necklace. "These are so beautiful! Thank you! Thank you! I have something for you too." She handed him a box that was also beautifully wrapped.

Mike tore into his package and found a two-piece heart pendant. He asked, "But why is it broken?"

Taking it from his hands, she clipped it together with the magnet inside and said, "It's broken only when it separates. So will our lives be."

They kissed and hugged.

* * *

A week later, they brought in the New Year together, toasting a new life as well. Rina continued living with Amir and helping to care for his children. It was a crazy, unusually cold winter with some snow and ice, but early spring finally arrived.

CHAPTER
TWENTY-ONE

Wednesday, March 4, 2048

After serving breakfast, Rina was getting ready to take Amir's children—a fifth-grade boy and a high school freshman girl—to school. As she handed them their lunches and light jackets, the house began to shake violently.

Amir Jr. let out a light scream and said, "Whoa! Aunt Rina, did you feel that? I think the house was trying to fly like the house in *The Wizard of Oz*. That was cool!"

"The mind of a child, so unlearned. I think someone hit the light pole at the end of the street again," Shira, his sister, said.

"I don't think so, Shira," Rina said. "I've experienced tremors before, and that was a serious one. Let's check the news before we leave, then I'll call Mike at his office to see what they recorded."

Just then, Rina received a call from Mike.

"Hello, Rina. Did you guys feel that? It was big for this area —4.4."

"We did. These kids are so funny. Amir Jr. thought it was cool. It was of a comparable magnitude to some I've felt in Seattle."

"Speaking of which, Mount Saint Helens has been acting up lately. Are you sure you want to go back there to live?"

"That's where my job is."

"Honey, I can get you on here. We had someone leave a couple of weeks ago. Besides, we're getting married in June, and I never thought of us living at the foot of a hot lava bowl either."

"Mike! Are you suggesting that we—"

"No, I'm not. You can get your own place, or Mom and Dad would be delighted to have a visitor for three months."

"Let me speak to Amir and his wife. They have a huge house. I'm still welcome here, and they would love that idea."

"This quake is a serious reminder of what I think we may be facing in the near future."

"If it's decided that I stay, I'll have to go and negotiate with my landlord about my lease agreement and pick up a few things. I don't have much."

"I've been looking at my schedule and appointments. Looks like Good Friday's a better time. I'll be off that day. Let me know what Amir and his wife say, and I'll clear it with Dad to use his jet and pilots."

"All right, I'll talk to you after you get off work. Goodbye."

"Talk to you then. Goodbye," Mike said.

* * *

On Monday morning, March 23, 2048, approximately two years after the Ring of Fire meeting, Misty Myers held another meeting with her science team via holographic telepresence.

Misty said, "First, let me say greetings to everyone. I have a few open seats just in case my supervisor, Dr. Nealson, manager, Dr. NaHony, and President Miles Duncan can join us at some point before we're finished. The floor is now open for any new discoveries, but if there are any unresolved issues from our last meeting, we'll address those first. Anyone who wishes may begin."

She checked the control board and said, "Yes, sir, the representative from Alaska. Please begin."

"Dr. Myers, I received notification of recent data reports and an explanation of all the apparent changes in the direction of the cracking or tunneling. If you will, can you elaborate?"

"Yes. Dr. Rina Adelstein, will you please share what we've discovered."

"Thank you, Dr. Myers, and greetings, everyone. In the past few months, data from three of our regional offices were analyzed and revealed that most of the runners or lead cracks seem to be channeling toward main faults. These fault runners, by the thousands, are now on a path toward major volcanoes and are moving at a rapid pace."

"Dr. Adelstein, just how many tunnels are connecting with these thousands of runners?" The Australian representative asked.

"From what our data reveals, it could be upward of tens of thousands to hundreds of thousands."

"Can the Earth stand that much separation?"

"The Earth's a very large mass, so it can stand it, but the quaking we've experienced is a result."

The Ecuadorian representative raised a hand and said, "My question is for Dr. Michael T. Lathan Jr. Sir, you implied at our last meeting that you're almost convinced that intelligent life could be responsible for these runners. With something now moving so rapidly and into the openings of volcanoes, wouldn't that sort of point toward lava movement?"

"One would be inclined to consider that, except for some geological facts," Mike said. "One is that, in most cases, lava is pushed almost straight upward from a lava pool. The movements in the recent months have not been consistent with that fact."

"And you said some geological facts—plural—but that was only one. What's another?"

"Lava doesn't have a season. Its upward movement is determined by pressure buildup. These movements have been occurring with a seasonal pattern. That's consistent with the habits of living creatures."

"What types of seasonal patterns?"

"Well, worldwide, birds fly south for the winter. In Africa, many migrations of animals are governed by weather changes. That's what I believe we're seeing here."

"Say that your suspicions are correct," the Yellowstone National Park representative said. "Wouldn't one be led to believe these migrating beings are moving toward their own demise? What life-form can live in the area of active lava? Wouldn't the seismic activity frighten them away?"

"It's a proven fact that scorpions can live through an atomic blast. Roaches can stand extremely hot climates and soil, even close to volcanoes," Mike answered.

President Duncan, Dr. Nealson, and Dr. NaHony joined the meeting. "Greetings, Dr. Myers and all other attendees," President Duncan said. "We've been listening blind and discussing your proposals. So tell me, Dr. Lathan, should we be concerned about scorpions and roaches, or should we be planning massive evacuations worldwide?"

"Mr. President, it's such a pleasure and an honor to have you join us," Mike said. Before he could respond to the question, the president continued.

"When Dr. Nealson and Dr. NaHony informed me of what would be discussed, I didn't want to miss out. So far, I've been intrigued with what I've heard, to say the least. Again, we're faced with some hard decisions, but there's no foreseeable timeline that can be applied to either scenario as to whether there are beings moving upward or lava."

"Our data does not strongly suggest lava because although some quaking and eruptions have been experienced, nothing has been consistent with major eruptions of the past," Mike proceeded.

"If I am going to have to issue a nationwide evacuation for volcanic regions, I need something more reliable," President Duncan said. "If you don't think communities are going to be threatened by eruptions and lava, what are you indicating we prepare for—nationwide pest control? Now, Dr. Lathan, I know your father very well, and I'm sure you have discussed this with him. What does he think?"

"Sir, with all due respect, my father believes that I am not only a good clergyman but also an excellent scientist. He respects my analysis without deeper input. He told me to believe in my work and be sure of my findings, and I do and I am. We do know something's moving upward. What that is, we have yet to see. As far as a time frame, it's not determined yet."

"Then what do you have to report that is definite?"

"Sir, our findings further support the possibility that communication is commencing through the tunnels—something similar to the sonar that whales or dolphins would use, but the patterns are different."

"What is the chance that the data is flawed?"

"Very low to not at all. If there were problems, we'd know it. Our systems are calibrated quarterly, sir."

"Well, based on the evidence I've heard, I'll need to meet with my advisors on these matters to determine what, if anything, is to be given to the public at this time. We appreciate all the hard work your teams are doing. I'm signing off with a big thank-you to everyone! Back to you, Dr. Myers."

"OK, everyone, look to hear from me or one of my team members," Misty said. "Keep monitoring and keep sharing data with each other and us. This session is over. Goodbye, everyone."

CHAPTER
TWENTY-TWO

Good Friday, April 3, 2048—10:45 a.m.
Mount Saint Helens

Mike called Rina to prepare for their flight to Seattle in his father's jet. They met the pilots at Dallas Love Field Airport and took off at 9:00 a.m.

"Buckle up, babe," Mike said to Rina. "It's going to be a good flight. I can tell. Skies are clear from here to the Seattle airport. We should be landing at around 11:15 a.m. Pacific standard time. Is this little jet going to be able to take off after we load your stuff in Seattle?"

"All right, Mike, I own about five suits and twenty days' worth of clothing changes."

"But that doesn't make sense. You're a woman."

"A conservative woman."

"I thank God for that. But I fear that will change in Dallas. My mom will make sure of it."

"Ooh! I love my mother-in-law already!"

"Really! She's gonna spoil you rotten, I'm afraid. You're going to be the daughter she never had but always thought about."

"I promise total control of my own spending habits."

"Uh-oh, you have a spending habit?"

"You know what I mean!"

"Yes, just kidding, hon. How much of a habit?"

"You know what I mean, Michael T. Lathan Jr.! I'll be working."

"For me, so it's still my money you'll be spending. But it'll be your right as my wife. Ha ha!"

"Yes, a big laugh is in order."

"So what color will you be wearing at the wedding?"

"There you go again. Should I wear black?"

"Black?"

"Sounds like it could be a funeral."

"OK! OK! No more jokes, I promise!"

They had breakfast and coffee on board.

"It's now 10:45 a.m., Mr. Lathan. Prepare for descent. We're approaching the airport," Ron, the pilot, said.

While circling Mount Saint Helens, they could see streams of black-and-gray smoke ascending from the volcano's opening. The smoke was so thick that they could not see until they reached a lower altitude.

Detrick, the copilot, said, "Did you feel that rush of wind that pushed us?"

Ron replied, "Yes, I did. The airport's approximately 147 miles, and we need to adjust our approach."

"What's going on? Is everything OK?" Mike asked Detrick.

"Yes, Mr. Lathan. We just need to adjust our descent, and we'll reach our proper approach altitude," Detrick answered.

Ron confirmed.

"Do you guys hear that? Sounds like Mount Saint Helens wants to blow her top again," Mike said.

"Yes, it was strange. More like burping, like she needs to throw up," Ron said.

"Well, our team of scientists has known for a while that something's been happening, but that's another issue."

At about that time, it appeared that the volcano shook.

The jet started its descent while banking near the top of the volcano, and a huge, black, smoky-looking cloud rapidly rose from the volcano's opening. There was a loud fluttering noise and immediately, the plane was peppered with what sounded like small stones. One of the engines sounded like a giant blender crushing ice and began to smoke.

Ron checked his gauges to note the status of that engine. He then heard a solid impact to the windshield and quickly looked to see a creature that resembled a nine-inch grasshopper. It had two sets of wings that fluttered like a hummingbird. The creature had the face of a man and long hair, and it appeared to have a gold crown on its head. Its body was shaped like that of a horse with an iron breastplate, its tail resembled that of a scorpion, and it had two hopper legs. When it turned and looked into the cockpit, it displayed lionlike teeth and seemed to growl.

Ron looked at Detrick and screamed, "What the hell is that?"

They both looked at the windshield again. It had disappeared.

Detrick looked like he was in shock. When he responded, he said, "I can't admit to what I saw. I just got this job. Besides, they'll test me and know I had a martini late last night."

Mike rushed to the cockpit.

"Guys, what's happening? Is everything OK? Why's the engine smoking like that? Can we land?"

"The engine appears to be OK. It's smoking a little, but the gauge shows it to be just fine," Ron said.

"What was all that noise all around the plane and in the engine?" Mike asked.

"This plane can fly on one engine, but we'll have it checked out when we land," Detrick said. "It appears that Mount Saint Helens is throwing rocks at us, small ones. But we're OK. We'll assess any damage while on the ground."

"This mountain is showing her bad side," Mike said. "How soon do you think we can take off for the return flight? It'll probably take about five hours to get all of Rina's stuff and return to the hangar."

"I can't be sure until we assess the damage," Ron said. "But we can make it home if it becomes necessary. There's a great team of techs and mechanics in Seattle. We'll be OK. We're in good hands. After we land, I'll contact your father and inform him of the problem."

"Don't worry about that. I'll take care of it," Mike said.

"Yes, sir."

* * *

The plane landed and entered the hangar. Mike rented an SUV, and he and Rina headed to her place to pack up her things. Afterward, they went to a deli to get a bite for lunch.

"Is the plane OK?" Rina asked. "I hope your dad won't be angry at me."

"Angry at you for what?"

"It's my fault we're here and the plane's damaged," Rina said.

"Don't worry about that. None of this is your fault. And we don't yet know how significant the damage to the plane is. Perhaps it's not as bad as it seemed. Let's finish lunch and head to the lab."

* * *

After lunch, they went to the University of Washington campus. Professor Dodds and his staff greeted Rina and Mike at the lab.

"Rina, how are you, dear? We've been so worried about you," Professor Dodds said.

"Considering the storms, I am well. Mike and I have settled on a date for our wedding. Which brings me to another issue—my job."

"Say no more about it. I—well, we, all of us here—love you and miss you, but we understand that life changes our circumstances. We've expected this day, and we kind of figured since Mike proposed to you that you probably would be moving."

"We will miss your smile, your kind nature, and your brilliance here at the lab, but yes, we expected it," an office coworker said.

"It would be foolish not to follow your heart, and we all know that Mike's your heart," Stacy said.

"Thanks to all of you," Rina said. "And I'll stay in touch. But maybe you all need to get out of Seattle as well. The spitting hill, as we sometimes call Mount Saint Helens, is not too stable lately. But we are on a tight schedule and must get back to the airport for our departure."

"Professor Dodds, it's good to see you again," Mike said. "Before we leave, can you tell us what's going on with the volcano?"

"Well, you know there's been a constant groaning within its bowels for quite some time, but we've picked up no extreme heat changes. It's the same story everywhere. Kind of strange, wouldn't you say?"

"Indeed so, sir," Mike said. "Well, it's time for us to get back. We'll keep in touch."

* * *

They returned to the airport hangar to find the pilots talking with mechanics and techs.

"So, what's the damage report like?" Mike asked.

"It's hard to believe, but there's no damage at all," A mechanic said.

"What about the smoking engine?"

"Actually, it was more like heavy dust of a carbon type, which is very strange because it's not consistent with smoke from a fire, especially volcanic fire or ash, but more of a carbon dust."

"Carbon dust? Exactly what does that mean, and what about the grinding noise coming from that engine?"

"Therein lies another mystery," a technician said.

"Mystery?" Rina asked. "What does that mean?"

"Well, from the grinding, we'd expected some leading-edge damage to several of the turbine blades, but there's not much more than finish scuffing," the technician said. "And the bypass duct was filled with that dust. There were signs of blood residue and hair strands, nothing else."

"Could it be birds or bats of some kind?" Rina asked.

"Not unless they have hair."

"Hair?" Mike asked. "What kind of hair? Did you keep any samples of either the hair or the carbon? And what about the blood?"

"You can probably find some samples on the floor in the wash bay where we cleaned the plane. The dust was all over it," the mechanic said.

"Do you have a jar or a plastic bag?" Mike asked.

"I've got a box of bags in that supply cabinet over there," the tech said. "I'll grab some for you."

"Thanks, I appreciate it."

Mike and Rina headed to the wash bay and got samples of the hair and some mushy samples of the carbon mixed with washing fluid. When they returned, Mike said, "I heard you guys talking about the smoke from the volcano. What was strange about it?"

"Well," the mechanic said, "when smoke rises, it's usually carried away with wind currents and disappears."

"What's strange about that?" Mike asked.

"About half the smoke was reported to have settled back to the ground on the volcano's surface," the tech replied.

"Well," Mike said, "the molecular makeup of carbon residue is heavier than that of fire-produced smoke. Nevertheless, it could be an interesting find. But in the bay, I found no traces of blood. There may be some answers there."

"I'm not sure if we have time for exploring," Rina said.

"You're right. We don't. We've got to get this bird back to its nest in Dallas. But I'm sure if there are answers up there, they'll be found soon. I can't wait to get back to the lab to analyze these samples."

"Mr. Lathan, may I speak to you in private?" Ron asked.

"Sure, let's step over there."

Detrick looked at Ron and said, "Sir, remember my job!"

Mike and Ron went outside the bay.

"Yes, what is it?" Mike asked. "Whoa! I wish you could see the look on your face. You saw something, didn't you? Come on, Ron, tell me what you saw. How about Detrick? Did he see it too?"

"I'm not sure of what Detrick saw, but I'm darn sure of what I saw. It was strange. I'm afraid for us all. If what I saw was in fact what I saw, we could be in for a world of hurt, all of us."

"When we get to Dallas, I want you to meet with—"

"No! No! I can't tell anyone else. They'll fit me for a straitjacket for sure!"

"I haven't heard you say anything about what you saw, but I believe you already. All I want you to do is meet with Dad and myself, OK? I'll do my best to keep your name clear. But if it turns out to be real, you could become an overnight celebrity, even a hero."

"A celebrity? A hero? Not a patient at a cuckoo farm?"

"You could be a part of history! Heck, all of us will be a part of history if it's what I've been thinking for some years now. Life will never be the same. Ever! All I will say is that I believe that you are a true Christian. If you weren't, you wouldn't be flying for Dad. But if there is anyone you know who is not, tell them to get born again now, if it's not too late."

"Sir, normally, that would either make me laugh or scare me silly.

But because of what I saw, I feel as though I'm already scared silly! I just hope I'm scared *enough*!"

"You'll be OK. Really."

"How can you be so sure? I'm afraid for the human race right now!"

"Well, for some, there's probably no real help outside of grace. Especially for those who may be walking a thin line."

"A thin line?"

"Just meet me at Dad's after we land."

CHAPTER
TWENTY-THREE

They arrived at Dallas Love Field Airport, and Dr. and Mrs. Lathan were there to meet them. They all went to the Lathans' home, and everyone went straight to Dr. Lathan's office except for Mrs. Lathan.

"Ron, I received a notification from the FAA about some problems with the plane. You want to tell me what happened?" Dr. Lathan asked.

"Uh . . . there was a problem when we were flying around Mount Saint Helens. Something was coming out of her mouth. Something that's hard to explain," Mike said.

"Hard to explain? Why don't you try being a little more specific, son?" Dr. Lathan asked.

"Dad, settle down. Your plane's OK. It was something out of the ordinary."

"I was certain that I asked you to be specific. Is this about your prediction?"

"There was no prediction, Dad, only proposals."

"Son! Are we going to have an intelligent conversation, or are we going to dance around facts all evening? I know this is not about the plane, so will someone please say something that is more direct!"

"Please, Dad, settle down. I believe that Ron has something interesting to say, and maybe Detrick does too. Something maybe even strange."

"OK, Ron, what's going on? No riddles, no parables, please. I've had enough of that for one day."

"Have you ever known me to be anything but serious?" Ron asked. "Well, I'm going to be *very* serious right now. As we were passing over Mount Saint Helens, something resembling smoke came out of the mouth of the beast mountain."

"Beast mountain? Mount Saint Helens? Uh, you kids. Please, go on!"

"It appeared to be charcoal smoke surrounding the plane. We began to be hit, hundreds of times, by something that sounded like small stones."

"Small stones? Yet there was no body damage?"

"I heard the left engine grinding loudly, and it appeared to be smoking."

"Smoking? Hmm. The hangar tech told the FAA there were no signs of heat or fire damage, so explain that one to me."

"Dad, I told you that it was strange."

"Michael! Strange halfway makes sense. There's *no* sense in what he just said! Have you been drinking, Ron? Have you been doing drugs?"

"See, what did I tell you, Ron?" Detrick said.

"So you did see something as well, didn't you?" Mike said.

"Sir, I was just afraid I'd lose this job."

"Son, telling the truth won't cost you your job, but telling a lie might. Not saying what you saw is as bad as saying that you didn't see anything when you and Ron both know you did," Dr. Lathan said.

"Don't both of you speak at once," Mike said. "However, one of you should start talking right now. Rina, why don't you go into the family room and keep Mom company."

"As a scientist, don't you think I should know what's going on?" Rina asked.

"OK, you're right. I'd like for you to stay."

"OK, thanks."

"Ron, please start."

"Yes, sir. As we banked into our descent, I saw what appeared to be very dark smoke exiting the mouth of Mount Saint Helens. As we flew through it, we were hit hundreds of times by something that I considered to be small stones. One hit the windshield rather solidly, so I looked for a sign of damage, but what I saw, or thought I saw— at first, I thought it to be a very, very large insect or grasshopper."

"A grasshopper? Coming out of a volcano!" Dr. Lathan said.

"That's what it looked like at first! You see, it had two hopper legs and four wings!"

"Hmm . . . Go on, Ron."

"It turned and looked at me, and I could see an angry scowl on its face."

"A scowling grasshopper? What else?" Mike asked.

"Sir, it appeared to have the body of a small horse, about eight to nine inches long, maybe three to four inches tall. Its tail looked like that of a scorpion."

"Detrick, is this what you saw?" asked Dr. Lathan.

"Yes, sir, exactly. Except also, its body appeared to be covered with some sort of plates, armor maybe. I could see teeth, like a lion's teeth, but its face, before it growled, looked like the face of a man, and it had long hair. On the top of its head appeared to be a golden crown."

Rev. Dr. Lathan, his frustrated expression now one of shock, looked at his son and then back at the pilots and said, "Thank you. I can understand why you were reluctant to share what you'd seen. You guys can go now."

"You believe us, don't you? Both of you?" Detrick asked.

"Guys, the look on your faces in the cockpit alone told a story. We just needed to hear it. Thanks again, and we'll talk later," Mike said.

The pilots, relieved that they still had a job, both left.

"Wow," Rina said. "I think I will go and keep your mother company now." She left the office.

"So a grasshopper that is part horse, lion, scorpion, and man, with long hair and dressed for battle. What does it mean? Mike, do you really believe this is what's been detected around the volcanoes and fault lines that's been causing all the quaking around the world?" Rev. Dr. Lathan asked.

"As a scientist, Dad, I'd say yes, but as a biblical scholar, I would dare to say that we're in for a rough ride for quite some time. In fact, I'm almost certain that it's a part of some worldwide campaign. But what and why would be easy to see but hard to say. My question is, has it begun?"

"I think maybe you answered your own questions during your last group conference. You talked of how this may in fact be the witnessing generation that experiences the ushering in of the end-time."

"How I wish and hope that I am wrong. Are we ready for it?"

"Will humankind ever be ready for it? No! But it is going to happen. Now or later only tells when, not if!"

"Dad, let's discuss the matter a little deeper. I've been looking into the prophecy in question a lot lately, and even I have questions."

"Not to sound facetious, but that's why I preferred your PhD to be in theology instead of science. Your course of study caused you to miss out on very necessary skills in biblical research and inter-pretation."

"Doesn't the Bible state that interpretations come from God?"

"It does record that statement, but does God verbally give us the interpretations, or does He give us the spiritually guided gifts and skills to be able to hear what's not verbalized or to see what's not drawn out?"

"So where is the shortcoming in my proposals?"

"Mike, I've not said it, but I've been with you all the way, studying your proposals and findings, doing my own biblical research. Now tell me, what do you believe is about to occur?"

"I believe that this is in fact the generation that will experience these things."

"Based on the events that have been taking place in recent years, it very well could be, whether we're ready for it or not."

"Another question that I have is this: What would be the purpose of the locusts, as they're called in the Bible, to sting just to hurt humans, not to kill them, for their disbelief?"

"There is a very visible fact that you're missing, son."

"Oh . . . well . . . OK, I'm learning."

"Remember, the Bible also states that these locusts will be commissioned, not just told, not to hurt any vegetation but to hurt man—but not unto death. The lesson here is that locusts hurt vegetation by not just landing on it but eating it until it dies, then moving on to the next stalk. By that fact, it is implying that these insects will be with us for five months, not eating vegetation. So how will they survive for this long without eating? The creatures are like so many others that have a certain season for storing fat and energy for off-season hibernation.

"Therefore, if they're not eating vegetation, their natural food, what will they eat? It's obvious that they'll be out of hibernation for at least five months. So again, how will they survive for that long of a period if they haven't eaten?" Dr. Lathan continued.

"I have a feeling you've got an answer," Mike said. But before you continue, let me share something that Rina told me a few days ago. When she was a teen, she had a dream in which creatures that resembled these, down to the teeth, came out of the sky and attacked people. About ten years ago before the hailstorm, while coming out of the lab, she saw strange-looking clouds in the sky and went into a trancelike state and saw angelic beings in the form of clouds floating around in the sky. One was blowing what looked like a horn, and others were just sitting in a patient-looking posture, looking as though they were waiting for their turns to blow their horns. This gave life to my theory. Now you can go on."

"Very interesting and very real. Now, to continue, the Bible further states that these creatures were commissioned to hurt men but not kill them. That's found in Revelation 9:5–6. These verses say that they'll torment men for five months and people will attempt suicide without success. Which leads me to believe that for five months, man will be their source of food."

"Dad, it doesn't say they'll feed on people. It just says they will sting them."

"OK, Mike, now put your scientist hat back on, and let me ask you this: Why do scorpions sting, for the most part? To subdue their prey, paralyzing it so it can't escape, or, better yet, so it can't fight back and injure the scorpion."

"So you believe that people will be stung to be rendered helpless to defend themselves. But to be fed upon? That's vague, Dad, wouldn't you agree?"

"To the unskilled, untrained mind. Ron and Detrick both saw teeth on the insect, teeth that looked like a lion's. Now, you're a scientist. Why are a lion's teeth made the way they are? To bite! Canines are for one purpose: to puncture and rip out chunks of meat. I do believe these creatures are commissioned to feed upon humans to torment, not to kill. Can you imagine it, how horrible it might get?"

"I can only hope we're missing the mark on our beliefs. If not, it will be a living nightmare."

"We should all pray, pray for each other and for humankind, that we all have the Mark of God!"

"Dad, what, if anything, can or will we take to the public?"

"We won't have to take anything to the public. I guarantee you the public will be going to the US government for answers!"

CHAPTER
TWENTY-FOUR

Good Friday, April 3, 2048—1:45 p.m.
Marshall County
West Virginia

Jan Brown of QUIK News began her breaking news report about attacks in a coal mine in West Virginia.

"Hello to all our viewers. We're coming to you with all of our sister stations around the world. Right now, we're going to our on-the-scene reporter, Robert Chance, in West Virginia, who is currently at one of the major underground coal mines. Hello, Robert, are you there?"

"Yes, Jan, this is Robert."

"Tell us what's happening there."

"Well, with me now is an eyewitness who'll tell us his story. This is Ramone, who's originally from South America but moved his family here for the work. So Ramone, tell the viewers what you experienced and saw."

"Our team was down the mine shaft about nine hundred feet. The boss said it was time for a break, so we were loading up our small tools on the elevator. Someone shouted that he could hear scratching inside the shaft wall on one side, so we got very quiet. We heard it too, but we thought it might be water or gas or something.

"A hole the size of a cart's wheel broke through, and we saw many, many eyes looking at us. Everyone who could fit on the elevator went straight up. I was one of those who had to wait for the elevator to come back down. Insects, big insects, came through the hole as it got larger, the size of a truck tire. They started stinging and biting many of the team. Men were cursing and screaming."

"Were you bitten or did any sting you, Ramone?"

"I thank my God, no. I kept my eyes closed, and I just prayed over and over, 'Lord, don't let them bite me. Lord, don't let them sting me.' When I came up on the elevator, the others said some insects had gotten into the elevator and stung and bitten the men all the way up. They went to the hospital, all of them. They said the insects flew away, and no one got a good look, only that they were very, very big. We could hear them because their wings made a very loud eerie noise."

"That's what I've been hearing others say," Robert said.

"Yes. I thank God I didn't get stung, didn't get bitten. I prayed. I kept praying. It sounds like they hurt really badly!"

"There you have it firsthand from Ramone, who was there but miraculously was not injured in any way," Robert said. "From the accounts given to us, he was very lucky, but he says he was blessed by God, who spared him. We don't know why so many were injured, but there were about twenty-two out of eighty workers who had no injuries, and they all claimed it was God who spared them the agony.

"No one seems to have gotten a good look at these insects because the dim light was filled with dust particles floating around. It's said that all the insects exited the shaft and flew away. Other witnesses say they've never seen insects that large, nor seen any fly so fast," Robert continued.

"We've received reports coming from one of the care flight pilots that it appears that the men had been fed on. He said that small chunks of skin and flesh had been ripped from the victims, with minimum amounts of blood loss. It didn't appear that the wounds were life-threatening, but they were serious because each person suffered so many bites. And there were holes the size of a large needle, oozing a yellowish, pus-like substance.

"The men complained of being stung and then being unable to move for about half a minute while they were literally being eaten by several of the insects. Some of the men said they thought they were going to die from the stings because they hurt so badly. These men were screaming and crying from the pain.

"There you have it, straight from ground zero," Robert concluded.

"Robert, thanks again," Jan said. "Are there any more reports from nearby areas that may have been attacked by the very large and very hungry insects?"

"We haven't heard of any just yet, but the nearby towns are bracing for invasion, whether it happens or not. This is Robert Chance reporting from West Virginia. Back to you, Jan."

"Thank you, Robert, and thank you, Ramone. Goodbye."

After the feed from the correspondent clicked off, Jan continued. "We have reports that Robert spoke with several workers who came up on the elevator with Ramone who didn't want to be interviewed because of their wounds. They were awful to say the least, he said. We're going to stay on the air for other reports that may come in. Hopefully, someone got a good look at these creatures, or large flying insects, if you will."

Good Friday, April 3, 2048—12:45 p.m.
Irving, Texas

Early Good Friday morning, a group of marathon runners met to run their usual thirteen miles to practice for an upcoming marathon. As they were finishing up, they neared the Fritz Park area in Irving, Texas. They continued down Shady Grove Road to Belt Line Road. The sun was bright and warm as they continued for another three and a half miles.

When they crossed I-30 and approached a small creek, they began hearing noises. They all looked toward the west side of the bridge over the creek and saw a dark cloud that was about fifty feet above the creek to the bottom of the bridge. The cloud was about six hundred feet from them. They could hear a loud noise that got louder as the cloud got closer.

When the cloud, which curved back around the creek as far as their eyes could see, got within about one hundred and fifty feet, they could see insects flying very fast toward them. The insects were soon upon them, and they ran into a wooded area for cover, screaming. One of them said, "They're just locusts. They're looking for grass."

But the locusts dove down on them, stinging and biting most of them. There were about two hundred runners. Most were already pretty tired and had problems picking up speed, but by the time they reached the woods, the locusts had overtaken them all.

The runners were on the ground, kicking at first, and then suddenly they were still, almost as if paralyzed, but they could still scream and cry. Some could only pant and breathe very rapidly while begging for relief. Seeing small chunks of skin and flesh being bitten from their bodies was causing many to go into shock.

There was nothing any of them could do. Suddenly, about forty runners simultaneously jumped up and began to swat the locusts from their comrades because they were not being attacked. They looked at one another and noticed a glowing light on their foreheads. Some had sweatbands on, but the light glowed through them. Realizing that they were not under attack and couldn't stop the attack on their friends, they screamed and yelled at the locusts in an attempt to scare them off. It was of no use though, so one young man grabbed one of the large locusts, and it turned and looked at him.

What he saw rendered him speechless. He just stared at it, and it growled, displaying its lionlike teeth.

Another young man screamed with fear, "Let it go! Run, run! If you can, get out of here now!"

The man who had grabbed the locust turned it loose and ran as fast as he could, then tried desperately to catch a ride. The drivers on the road thought there might be something wrong with him because he looked totally deranged, and they were afraid to stop for him.

He yelled, "In the woods, in the woods, they're being attacked! My friends are being eaten alive!" But no one would stop.

He picked up a bat-size branch and ran back toward the woods to find that the locusts had gone. The runners started moving around. He could see many were injured. Some had at least fifteen bite marks, notches in their skin about the size of a dime, not too deep, but serious. He was concerned they might get rabies or something similar.

He and others got on their cell phones. Some called family members, others called for professional medical help, and some called the local police. All those who had not been attacked gathered in a huddle to discuss the event. They noticed that there was a common factor they all shared: markings on their foreheads that glowed. Some glowed brighter than others; some were barely notice-able. They all were surprised by the markings. Some said they had noticed them some time ago. They began to question the victims to see if anyone else could identify what the locusts looked like. No one said anything, other than a young man who stated that when the locusts had dived down toward them, they just ran—ran like hell.

The first responders to arrive were two state troopers who were in the area on I-30 when the call came in. One trooper, a bald man, asked, "Can anyone tell me what these insects looked like? Anyone? Come on, now. Someone had to see."

"Officer, it was quite frightening to see that many locusts flying down toward you. They were huge and very strange looking. Locusts don't just attack and eat people. They eat grass. These things were not just biting; they were feeding. I'm a total mess. My fiancé will probably back out of our engagement now," a woman said.

"Ma'am, you said that they were feeding on you all?" the second trooper said.

"Why didn't you keep running?" the bald trooper asked.

The woman, who was still crying and in pain, said, "It was sort of strange. They would sting first. After I felt the sting, my legs wouldn't respond to my thoughts. I wanted to run, sure enough, but I couldn't. It was as though I was paralyzed."

"What did the sting feel like? Was it like a bee, maybe, or a wasp or something like that?" the second trooper asked.

"More like an electrical shock," the woman said. "A few years ago, I plugged an appliance into a socket. I didn't know it had an exposed wire, and I got shocked. I couldn't turn it loose because I was momentarily paralyzed. It finally knocked itself out of my hands. That's what I felt, an electric-like shock and momentary paralysis."

"Where were you stung?"

"On the back of my neck, my back, my legs, my arms, and on my left hip."

"Let me see . . . Yes, I can see the holes. They're huge! I'm calling the paramedics right away."

At about that time, a young man approached the troopers. He asked the bald trooper, "Officer, may I speak to you in private?"

"Sure thing. Let's step over here by the bridge. What's on your mind? What did you say your name is?"

"Carl, sir. I'm Carl Smith. I put this run together."

"Mr. Smith, what do you have?"

"Well, it's more like, what did I see."

"OK then, what did you see?"

"Not only did I see, but I touched."

"You touched and you saw. Tell me, what did you experience?"

"Do you believe in science fiction?"

"You saw and touched science fiction?"

"That's the only explanation for what I saw!"

"Come on out with it, son."

"They sounded weird and made a really loud noise."

"Do I need to give you a sobriety test? Are you using these people's misfortune to get some attention? If you have something we can use, let's have it. If not, we need to get these people some help."

"OK, Officer, you asked for it. I grabbed one of those things that was biting a girl and had a hard time pulling it loose. These things were big, I mean really big."

"How big?"

"Eight to nine inches long, with two sets of wings. I grabbed it by the wings at first and thought the wings would break. I pulled as hard as I could, but the wings didn't break. They felt like silk, but they left black dust in my hand. So I grabbed it by its body. It felt like I grabbed an armadillo or something. But it turned its head and looked at me and growled!"

"Growled? Son, I'm gonna have to take you to the station to get your statement. Wow! No wonder you weren't attacked! Even locusts have better sense than to bite someone who's been smoking, which you apparently have been. Now, no one else saw or touched what you did. No one else saw or touched science fiction! I'll bet this'll get even better at the station. Let's go. Dave, can you handle this from here? I've got a real live wire!"

The second trooper, Dave, said, "Sure thing, Phil. I can see Irving city officers and the fire department coming. Go ahead!"

Carl told his story again in more detail at the station.

CHAPTER
TWENTY-FIVE

Good Friday, April 3, 2048—11:45 a.m.
Yellowstone Volcano Observatory, Wyoming

Misty made a phone call to the Yellowstone Volcano Observatory.

"Good afternoon, Carla, this is Dr. Misty Myers. I am the Program Coordinator/Volcanologist at the US Geological Survey office in the Volcano Hazards Program in Reston, Virginia."

"Yes, Dr. Myers. I remember you from the meeting in Reston. How can I help?"

"Have you guys been keeping up with the breaking news reports about activities inside and outside volcanoes around the world, especially the activities of the most dangerous ones? Do you have anything on tape there?"

"Let me take a look at our previous recordings from our mobile cams." After a pause, Carla, the Scientist-in-Charge, said, "Well, there's not much out of the ordinary . . . Wait, I see something around Biscuit Basin that appears to be smoke, very heavy smoke, accompanied by a loud noise. Whoa, that was strange!"

"What was strange, Carla? What did you see?"

"Well, the smoke, uh . . . Wait, it's not smoke but insects, very large flying insects that formed a big cloud. Huge! It appears to have broken up, and the insects flew in several directions. Oh my! More and more of them. Could be tens of thousands of them. What's going on, Dr. Myers? This is very strange."

"I can't say right now. I need to speak with my team's best researcher. Did the cam record whether any people or animals were attacked? And what time did all this happen?"

"It appears to have been around 11:45 a.m. There was a loud boom, and then a very dark cloud of smoke blocked out the cam recorder screen for some time. Wait—these were insects, Dr. Myers? Not bats?"

"Don't be surprised by the possibilities looming, Carla. There are many! I'll call the ranger station and check with them. Who's the on-duty ranger right now?"

"Well, let me see. The enforcement ranger on this shift is Donald Makings.

"Give me that number, will you?"

"I'll just transfer you. Hang on."

The phone rang. Then a woman answered. "Hello, this is Judy Aimes, Deputy Scientist-in-Charge. Can I help you?"

"This is Dr. Misty Myers from the Reston, Virginia, office. Is Ranger Makings at the station now?"

"He's on duty, but he's out in the park area. Some of the animals were a bit off their best behavior. Something seems to have caused them to run all over the park, with some desperately trying to leave their enclosures. They seemed spooked, but they did settle down after about an hour."

"Could you tell if there was any reason for their skittishness?" Misty asked.

"So far, I'm not totally sure, but Ranger Makings will be back in about three hours. He's scouring the park in the helicopter."

"If he reports anything at all, please have him call me at my office, OK?"

"I'll do that for sure, ma'am."

"It's very important that he calls me. Thanks. Goodbye."

Good Friday, April 3, 2048—7:45 a.m.
Mauna Loa volcano
Hilo, Hawaii

In the city of Hilo, Hawaii, located near the Mauna Loa volcano, the city manager, Adalia Lee, was sitting at her desk sipping her coffee. She called for her secretary, Arelia, to come into her office.

"Arelia," she said, "this is the big day. Do you have the report I asked for ready?"

"I'm almost done. I just need to set a couple more things for the hula dance, then the hula contest, and then I'll get it to you. The weather appears as though we'll get Mother Nature's approval."

"How many dance groups do we have committed so far?"

"All twelve that signed up have committed."

"That's wonderful."

Just then, Adalia's phone rang. When she answered, she heard the frantic voice of her son on the other end. He was a science student at the University of Hawaii at Hilo.

"Hello, Agrasha," Adalia said. "What's wrong? Slow down, son, and talk to me."

"Mother, has your dance festival started?"

"No, son. Why?"

"You should cancel now! There are reports that giant locusts are coming out of Mauna Loa and attacking people, even eating their flesh! Mom, don't go out there, OK? We've been getting strange readings at our seismic lab for about a week now. We didn't know what it was at first but thought it might be an eruption, given the history. The Christians around campus have been at their doom teachings here lately anyway. I'm watching the news, and it's bad. People are being told to stay indoors. These things are trying to get into buildings and homes. It won't be long before they'll be there, so please stay indoors until we get a handle on this mess. I'll call back when I have some answers, OK? Goodbye."

"OK, son, I'll wait for your call," Adalia responded.

She turned on the news and saw that he was right.

Good Friday, April 3, 2048—12:45 p.m.
Galeras volcano
Pasto, Colombia

Julio, a courier for a human trafficking organization, was en route to deliver a van full of underage girls—about twenty, who had been crowded into a long-bed Chevy van—to his boss at a factory warehouse in Pasto, Colombia.

Just as Julio arrived at the warehouse parking lot, the air was filled with a very dark smoke, and he could hardly see or breathe. He received a call from his boss, who was inside the warehouse on the second floor in a closed office. He asked Julio if he heard the Galeras volcano making a lot of noise.

"While opening the warehouse shipping door, I heard something," Julio said as he gasped for air. "Then suddenly, the air became filled with some sort of dust. I can hardly see or breathe."

At that moment, a swarm of giant locusts began attacking all the men and women at the factory warehouse. People who were being stung began falling into the aisles and behind boxes.

Julio had lied to the girls about where he was taking them, and the locusts swarmed him first, stinging and then biting and eating his flesh.

One of the young girls, Maria, asked another, "What's happening? What's happening, Sandra? Do you know?"

"All I know is that God is delivering us from this animal! Get back into the van, everyone. Come on, I can drive! I can drive!"

All the traffickers were being stung and bitten by locusts; therefore, they didn't notice the van leaving.

When Julio recovered enough to stand, he reported the incident to his boss, who became furious and said, "You let all the girls escape. That's not acceptable. Unless you get me another group, you're going to be held accountable. Do you understand? Someone had better get my van back. The police had better not trace it back to me."

"But boss, it wasn't our fault! We were attacked by biting and stinging locusts. We need to go to the hospital."

"You stay put. All of you. I'll get my doctor here. Nobody leaves."

"Please tell the doctor to hurry. We're bleeding badly!"

Good Friday, April 3, 2048—7:45 p.m.
Mount Vesuvius
Naples, Italy

About five miles east of Naples, Italy, in the gulf sits Mount Vesuvius, one of the world's most active and dangerous volcanoes. Simultaneously with other volcanoes around the world, loud booming and hissing began to emanate from Mount Vesuvius, and smoke filled the air. Within the smoke, a loud fluttering sound could be heard all the way to downtown Naples.

As Francesco Vincenzo was locking up his private law office, he heard the noise and looked upward toward the gulf to see what appeared to be a black cloud, a very large one, moving rapidly toward the downtown area. He hurried across the street to a rather crowded outdoor restaurant, where he was meeting his brother, Luigi, who was waiting at a table.

As Francesco sat down, he asked, "Luigi, do you see that? What in the hell is it?"

"Mama would scorn you for that kind of language, and you know I'm right. Are you going to Mass tonight?" Luigi asked.

"As much as I'd like to, I don't have time for that. I've got a hot date! I'm not as committed as you, Brother. Don't say a word. I know one day Saint Peter's going to frown on me, but I think maybe he and Mother Mary will forgive me!"

Francesco took a good look at his brother and asked, "What's wrong with your forehead? It looks like a neon light is flashing under the skin. Flashing an SOS, ha ha!" He looked at the sky and said, "Does it look to you like the smoke is getting lower? And what is that awful sound? It's so nerve-racking!"

"Cover your drink, quickly! That's not a cloud. It's insects!"

Francesco came under vicious attack and screamed in agonizing pain, being stung and bitten many times.

"Luigi, help! It hurts terribly! Help!"

He went silent and fell to the ground under the table. Luigi tried desperately to knock some of the locusts off Francesco, but they wouldn't fly away. They bit and devoured his flesh for over a minute, about five of them.

Luigi screamed frantically for help, but everyone who wasn't being attacked just ran. Many of them were not aware of the glowing on their foreheads.

The locusts suddenly flew away. As suddenly as they had attacked, they stopped. Police arrived at the scene and began questioning any witnesses they could find. About twenty-five people had been attacked at the restaurant, and many on the street had suffered as well. Officers were taking notes as reporters showed up.

Good Friday, April 3, 2048—7:45 p.m.
    Cairo, Egypt

Weeks before the Israelis were to celebrate their Passover, millions of locusts were seen flying over Cairo, Egypt. News reporters and their camera crews captured the events on video and in photographs. Many people were out dining, and things were almost back to normal after the locust encounter that had occurred weeks earlier.

Suddenly, the sky was filled with what looked like black smoke in the form of a great cloud. Two men were walking among the buildings, and as the cloud drew closer, they could see that these were locusts, not smoke.

"Why are these locusts appearing again?" Jabre asked. "They already migrated through our city weeks ago. I thought that was over."

"Yes," Aharon said. "They came through here and destroyed so much of our crops and vegetation that we're just barely getting back to normal."

The cloud of locusts began to break up and fly in different directions. Several people who were outside in downtown Cairo saw the swarms and began running, trying to get inside buildings, stores, or wherever they could find shelter.

Berenike saw some of them coming toward her and started running. She looked behind her and saw that these locusts were larger than normal and strange looking. As they attacked a man running behind her, she got an even better look at one and ran inside a store, shutting the door quickly behind her.

"Don't open the door! Those aren't insects! Those are demons!"

she cried to the store manager.

A man in the store put his face to the glass door to get a better look, and several flew into the glass in an attempt to attack him. He fell backward to the floor and just stared with shock. The manager ran over to him, knelt down, and asked, "Sir, are you OK? What did you see? Sir?" He yelled for someone to call the police.

The man sighed and said, "They can't help us, and they're in trouble as well. These creatures should not exist in our lifetime. Something very strange is happening. I don't know what it is, though." He looked over at Berenike and said, "Well, it doesn't look as though you were injured, ma'am. That's good. What did you see?"

She looked into his eyes and said, "I saw what you saw."

"I'm a scientist, but I'm not really sure what I saw," He responded. "But we should definitely wait until they're gone before we go out there."

Good Friday, April 3, 2048—7:45 p.m.
  Mount Nyiragongo
  Goma, Democratic Republic of the Congo, Africa

Rishi and his sister, Keicha, lived in Goma, Democratic Republic of the Congo, Africa. They were teens who were about to reach adulthood and were responsible for raising their four younger siblings. They were returning from checking their fishnets; it was a very good catch that evening. It was now starting to get dark.

"We must hurry to reach Goma's edge. We can't be on this trail at dark. Let's move faster," Rishi said.

"I can still see the great Mount Nyiragongo's peak. We have a little while yet before total darkness is upon us," Keicha said.

"Do I need to carry some of your catch for you so that you can move faster?"

At 7:45 p.m., a loud hissing came from the volcano and then a boom and another, then another. The ground shook, and Keicha fell to her knees.

"Are you all right? Are you hurt anywhere?" Rishi asked.

"No, I'm not hurt. Let's hurry, Brother!"

"Here, give me your two large fish, and you take my two small ones. Now let's run as fast as we can, Sister!"

A large swarm of insects flew over their heads about treetop high, moving toward their village. They ran even faster for fear their siblings were being attacked.

As they entered their hut in their small village, Rishi asked, "Are you all well? Where's Elonga and Elombe, the little ones?"

"We're fine!" Alongi said. "I covered the little ones with a blanket. We're all fine, but the insects came! Very big ones! They were stinging with their tails and biting several people. I watched from the opening in the wall. I was terrified."

Good Friday, April 3, 2048—8:45 p.m
Mount Suswa
Between Nairobi and Narok, Kenya

A group of tourists was on a guided tour near the Mount Suswa volcano located between Nairobi and Narok, Kenya. The volcano was unique in that it had a double crater. Some of the tourists had requested that the tour guides break the norm and tread through areas filled with dangerous wild animals to get closer.

The tour guides were all Maasai homesteaders who were brothers and lived around the base of the mountain. They discussed the matter among themselves, and one stated, "It's their money, and they'll pay special fees."

The head guide and elder brother, Kiano, thought it was too dark and advised against going any farther until morning. All the tourists, about twenty-five total, were lodged in open-windowed cabins having six to seven rooms each.

Kiano was roomed with his four brothers: Kairu, his close assistant and spokesman; Gacoki, the translator; and Jaramogi and Irungo, who were both former soldiers and guides. As they discussed the possibility of going off the regular tour route, Kiano was not pleased with the idea. He stated that the mountain was unusually busy that evening, noting the noisy growling and trembling. Kairu reminded him that there was no record of the mountain ever erupting, even though the trembling seemed more intense than ever.

"Brother, I know that it would be far from the ordinary if any bad thing occurred, but I've got a bad feeling in my stomach," Kiano said.

"I can explain that one easily, brother. I've eaten at your wife's table," Jaramogi said.

"With that kind of talk, it will be a cold day in hell before I invite you back," Kiano responded.

"Come on, you know it's true. That's why you're so angry all the time."

"Not nearly as angry as I'm getting."

The other brother, Irungo, interrupted, saying, "Silence, the both of you!"

They started the tour and after a short distant decided not to go any farther and returned to camp. A loud boom rang out from the crater, and the Earth shook violently.

"Kairu! How long has it been, you say?" Gacoki asked.

"It's never happened, and it won't erupt now," Kairu said. "We've seen this before, about five years ago. It wasn't serious then, and it's not serious now! So go to sleep!"

Some of the tourists approached the brothers' cabin, and Kairu went out and assured everyone that nothing was going to happen.

Suddenly, a noisy sound like a gust of wind could be heard in the dark, and screams began to ring out. There were cries of pain and profanity.

Someone cried, "I can't see anything, but something is biting and stinging me."

Half the tourists and three of the brothers were under attack. A flashing glow could be seen on the foreheads of the others. The attack lasted for about two and a half minutes, and the group was helpless to stop it. Some ran into their cabins and others tried to take refuge in the bus that had brought them, but no one could find the keys in the frantic scene.

As those who were not attacked tried to help, the onslaught suddenly ended, and only moaning and cries could be heard. Kiano contacted the head of the family who oversaw the tourist events. He reported the incident, asking for medical assistance for the injured.

April 4, 2048—12:45 a.m.
Mount Merapi
Yogyakarta, Indonesia

In Yogyakarta, Indonesia, a woman was awakened by a loud boom. She yelled out, "Guntur! Guntur! Come on, don't play sleep with me. Awaken, awaken, I say, right now. I'm so afraid!"

"Chahaya, you know not to wake me so early!" Guntur yelled. "It's barely past midnight! What's so important, wife, darn it! I just finished the tally for the rice crop. I'm so sleepy. What is it?"

"Husband, I heard a big noise from Mount Merapi. He sounds angry. See, you should have told the customer that most of the crop you sold him was withered."

"Not my fault. God has not blessed our efforts this year! It cost me the same to plant."

"But you should have been truthful. You should not mislead!

That's all I'll say."

"Woman, you do not know the ways of business! Let me deal with buyers my way! OK?"

"Well, I hear it. God's not pleased!"

"Will God feed us if I tell the truth? No! I think not!"

"Did you give him a chance? No! He's not pleased. He won't bless our harvest next time either."

"What do you hear, anyhow?"

"I screamed to you two times, and you did not hear. Mount Merapi screamed at you two times too. He didn't shake you like I did! I heard a loud, strange sound too, over our home."

"Do I need a baby's rattle to put you back to sleep? Do I? Or can you just go back to sleep? I can!"

The city of Yogyakarta was in for a rude awakening.

April 4, 2048—2:45 a.m.
Mount Sakurajima
Kagoshima, Japan

The Mount Sakurajima volcano could be seen across the bay from the city of Kagoshima, Japan. As Azuma and his two children—Chi, his twelve-year-old son, and Achika, his nine-and-a-half-year-old daughter—prepared to board Azuma's seventeen-foot boat to get an early start on some bay fishing, the mountain appeared to shake.

His son noticed it and shouted, "Whoa! Father, you saw that, didn't you?"

"Saw what, Chi?" Azuma asked.

"The hill shook. It shook very fast," Achika said. "I saw it, I promise, I saw it! Father, I pray all the time that it does not ever erupt again. Grandfather told us stories of how horrible it was the last time —1914, I think."

"Yes, my father told us that story a million times, and I've expected it to happen again," Azuma said. "Thank God it never has and probably never will. It's always shaking and roaring, like Father when he was angry."

They gathered all the equipment, including lanterns and loaded it onto the boat.

Azuma told Chi, "Son, start the engine. Let's get going. Can't wait to see what our catch will be today. The weather is great."

At that moment, the mountain blew a great black cloud from its top, resembling an atomic bomb going off. At first, Azuma considered going out anyway but changed his mind.

Suddenly, a loud sound like a strong gust of wind deafened their ears as the cloud quickly approached them.

"Get under the coats and cover yourselves. Don't look up until I say so, OK? Now, Chi, now!"Azuma shouted.

"Father, there's something on your forehead that's glowing. What does it mean?"

"Son, do as I ask. Cover yourself now!"

Azuma looked up and saw a cloud of giant locusts flying toward the city's downtown area. After the locusts passed them, he said, "We'd better cancel today and get home quickly. I don't know what's going on. I must check the news."

By the time they had loaded their gear back into their car, Azuma could hear screams and crying coming from seemingly everywhere. Driving through downtown, he could see the locusts attacking people.

"How strange this is. I've never seen locusts attack people. It's very strange. Not one has even so much as looked in our direction," he told his children.

"I think maybe Jesus wouldn't let them. That's what my church school taught us. Now I know it's the truth. He will save us if we love Him and each other," Achika said.

"Yes, He will, and yes, He did, I believe," Azuma said.

CHAPTER
TWENTY-SIX

Good Friday, April 3, 2048—Early Evening
Johnston Ridge Observatory
Seattle, Washington

All the world news channels were reporting loud echoes, all of which were taking place simultaneously, from major volcanoes in their areas.

Professor Dodds gave Rina a call.

"Hello, Professor Dodds. What's wrong? You guys missing me already? Well, I miss you as well."

"Yes, Rina, but that's not why I called. I want to take a team to the Johnston Ridge Observatory and do some investigating. Nothing's showing up on our data that would suggest a present danger as of yet. I know there's been smoke and a lot of noise at Mount Saint Helens, but maybe it's just the release of some trapped gas pockets. Has Dr. Myers or any of the team members come up with anything yet?"

"I haven't heard of anything. Maybe Mike has. I'll check with him. But you guys should be very careful. Mike's theory may point to something quite different than a full-scale eruption, yet it could be just as dangerous."

"Dangerous? In what way?"

"He feels there's enough evidence that some sort of life-form may be causing all the noise and some of the quaking."

"But what of the smoke that was reported exiting the mouth of the mountain's crater? By the way, where's Mike? Is he there with you?"

"No, actually, I'm at Amir's, but I'll call him if you'd like."

"Well, if you have a chance, but it's not critical. We're planning to go up as soon as I can get the team together."

"I'll try to reach him, but I'm not sure it's wise to go up there just yet. Have you been watching the news from around the world?"

"Yes, I've been keeping up with the news, but the quaking's not that severe here. I think we'll be all right. The observatory is in a safe location. Besides, I would love a closer look."

"If you must go, please pick a team of Christian researchers."

"Christians? What's that all about?"

"You're a Christian, aren't you, Professor?"

"Don't get spooked, Rina, but yes, I've been born again most of my adult life. But why do you ask?"

"I trust Mike's hunch. Remember, only Christian researchers. You don't want to put anyone in harm's way."

"Harm's way! Being a Christian won't save anyone from a major eruption, which I don't think will happen."

"Promise me or don't go. OK?"

"All right, all right! Can you give me the names of some of your close associates and ex-lab students?"

"Sure, I'll email you a list of names. Talk to you soon."

"Great. I'll wait for the email. Goodbye, dear."

* * *

Professor Dodds chose his team from the list of names Rina emailed to him, and soon thereafter, they were on their way up to the observatory.

When they arrived, Professor Dodds said, "OK, everyone, let's unpack our gear and have a quick snack. Afterward, we'll go down to the lava crust and take samples of the smoke or dust or whatever it is that's settled around here."

"What happened up here?" Bob, a student, asked.

"Earlier today, Dr. Rina Adelstein and Dr. Michael Lathan Jr. flew in and noticed smoke coming from the mouth of the crater. A technician at the airport hangar eighteen miles away said he noticed that instead of floating away, most of the smoke settled around the mountain. As we were landing a short while ago, from the copter, it looked like the lava bed was moving."

"But Professor, that's dead lava rock!"

"Yes, I know. It seemed strange, but maybe it was just an illusion from the sunlight. Normally, I'd split the team into two groups, but it may be wise for us to stay together. Stay close, OK?"

Professor Dodds conferred with the on-duty tech about any pending danger, but none had yet to be observed. Half an hour later, they exited the observatory and started exploring the grounds, looking into cracks and separations both large and small.

After about an hour, approximately a quarter mile down the slope, a loud noise emanated from several cracks. All around the team, locusts began to emerge. They flew upward about thirty feet, swarmed in a circular pattern, and then dove downward on the team.

As they all covered their faces in horror, only one of the eight team members was attacked. The others and Professor Dodds looked on in shocked amazement as the young man screamed out in pain and fell to the ground. He then went silent, and the locusts continued to bite and sting him over and over.

Jody, another student, snapped into action and yelled, "We've got to help Tom! They're biting and stinging him! I can see blood!"

He swung his flashlight back and forth as dozens of insects attacked the young man. The other team members made it to Tom and began sweeping at the creatures with their forearms. After about fifteen seconds, the creatures flew away.

"Son, are you OK?" Professor Dodds asked. "Someone get me that medic kit. He's been chewed rather severely."

Jody handed Professor Dodds the kit, and the professor began to administer first aid. Tom screamed out in pain.

"I know it burns, but it's necessary until we can get you to the hospital," Professor Dodds said.

* * *

At the hospital, the local police arrived. An officer approached Professor Dodds and asked, "Sir, is the patient one of your students?"

"Yes, he is. How is he?"

"The nurse says he'll be fine. What happened to him?" the officer asked.

"It happened so fast. We were about twenty yards apart when we heard him scream and saw these large grasshoppers all over him, stinging and biting him."

"No, sir!" Jody said. "They were eating him!"

"Insects don't eat humans. Heck, most don't even eat meat," the officer said.

"These do. They did. I saw it! It was terrible, man! I saw that everyone had a fluorescent glow on their foreheads—everyone except Tom. And I saw that I also had the glow when I used the restroom here to clean myself up."

"Who is Tom?"

"He's the one who got eaten on!"

"No one got eaten on, son."

"Officer, I'm telling you, they were eating him, and they weren't insects."

"Everyone else says they saw locusts, black locusts."

"I knocked one over and saw its face, and its teeth looked like canines."

"Are you sober, kid. Locusts don't have canines?"

"Sir, I'm a true Christian. I don't drink and I don't smoke either! I know what I saw. It had teeth like a lion and long hair. If that was a locust, it's a government experiment or it's been doing steroids."

"If you insist on telling that story, I'll let you finish it at the police station, where you'll be tested for substance use."

"It's OK, Officer," Professor Dodds said. "Jody, wait for me with the others in the lobby." He then told the officer he had to make a quick call and contacted Mike.

"Professor Dodds, hello, sir!" Mike said. "I'm surprised to hear from you so soon. What's going on?"

"Mike, have you spoken with Rina lately? She explained your theory and proposal to me a little while ago, and I was quite indifferent at the time, but now I'm much more serious. I was on an expedition with some of my students around the Johnston Ridge Observatory near Mount Saint Helens, and my team was attacked by large locust-looking creatures. One was seriously bitten, but it's not life-threatening."

On Mike's end, a news flash came on the monitor.

"Hold on just a moment, will you, Professor? I'm trying to see what's happening on the news . . . OK, yes, seems like they're talking about that incident and others like it in nearby towns and states—actually, all over the globe."

"Wow, I just heard a loud noise from the mountain. I'm stepping outside to take a look." Professor Dodds went outside. "Oh! Wow, Mike, this is incredible. A huge cloud of smoke just blew out of the top of Mount Saint Helens and blocked out the sun, and there's lots of darkness. The cloud is swirling around like a whirlwind, and now there are strange sounds. I think I'll go back inside until it clears up."

"Professor Dodds, listen to me. Yes, go back inside. Please don't go back out. I'm listening to the news flashes from all over the world. The same thing is happening everywhere in different locations. They're saying that it's not smoke coming out of the volcanoes but flying creatures, and they are moving into populated areas and attacking people the same way your team member was attacked!"

"That's the strangest thing. I've never known or heard of insects feeding on humans, but these things were literally biting and stinging the skin and flesh from this kid's body!"

"Did anyone get a good look at them? Good enough to describe them?"

"One of the students, Jody, did, and explained to the police that they were very large locusts that had teeth like a lion and long hair."

"Oh wow! If you hear anything else, please give me a call, will you?"

"Sure will, Mike. Talk to you later. Goodbye."

CHAPTER
TWENTY-SEVEN

Good Friday, April 3, 2048—Late Evening

Misty called Mike, after talking to Judy, who was stationed at the Yellowstone Volcano Observatory. "Hello, Misty, how are you?" he said.

"Have you been listening to the news reports? Have you and Rina been informed of the things going on in Yellowstone and near Mount Saint Helens?"

"That I have, for certain. As a matter of fact, I was speaking with Professor Dodds while he was at a hospital after one of his students was attacked. Also, Rina and I just got back from Seattle, Washington, and encountered something while circling Mount Saint Helens, something that the pilot and copilot saw that gives substance to my theory."

"Did you or Rina see anything at all?"

"No, but I'd like to go back up there to investigate what happened to Professor Dodds's student during their expedition around the base of the volcano. There's a lot I need to see. And I need to finish my testing of some samples I brought back from Washington."

"Yes, we do need those results, but as for Mount Saint Helens, I've got a team headed up there as we speak. What I would like for you to do is go to the observatory at Yellowstone Park. I was told that some recordings of interest warrant our attention. One of the mobile cams picked up a swarm of very large insects circling the enclosures, and I'd like your personal opinion. Thank your theory for that.

"It appears that this is the same type of insect that's been reported to be attacking and tormenting people all over the world, but only a couple of men actually got a good visual. One is a runner in Irving, Texas, but the local police are calling him a sci-fi nutcase. The other one's story has yet to be released. You be careful and get yourself one of those Kevlar protective suits. We don't want anything to happen to you."

"I'm on my way as soon as I can get a flight first thing in the morning."

* * *

The next day, Mike's plane landed at the airport in Wyoming. He had a team of four besides himself. Despite her vigilant efforts to accompany them, he had convinced Rina that she could serve them better by staying home near the phone.

When they got to the observatory, he could see a dark cloud circling an area, and he knew what to expect. They were greeted by Carla, who told Mike that Donald Makings, the enforcement ranger, would be assisting them. While waiting for Ranger Makings to return to the station, Carla showed Mike all the recordings that were available.

"Wow! They are huge, aren't they? And there seem to be

hundreds of thousands, if not millions, and in one concentrated area. Interesting!"

Ranger Makings called the observatory. "Ranger Makings," Carla said.

"Did our guests arrive yet?"

"Yes, they're here waiting."

"OK, I'll send a truck. Goodbye."

"Mike, he's sending a truck for you and your team," Carla said.

The truck arrived and took the team to an area, where Mike set up his portable lab for research and testing.

"While you're setting up, I'm going just over the hill there to pick out a good place to start," Ranger Makings said to Mike, pointing to the area.

"Well, I was hoping to start where the insects were recorded."

"That's a pretty dangerous hot spot right now. Different wolf packs border the ranges there. We'll move about three miles west of that one."

"OK, let's get started."

"Do you guys have protective suits? If not, I've got some available. They should fit."

The team soon arrived at the location and set up.

"OK, guys," Mike said. "We'll break up into three groups. Bill and Steve, you two go east toward those cliffs. Buddy and Sarah, I want you to go back over the hill, west of where we climbed to halfway down, and check those ground cracks. Ranger Makings and I will check out the caves here on the map down south, about one and a half miles across the trout stream."

"But first, Mike, I have to check out some poachers we were told about. I'll catch up to you in about an hour and a half," Ranger Makings said.

"Mike, Rina made me promise not to let you out of my sight!" Buddy said.

"Well, we can't let Sarah go by herself, can we? Besides, the ranger will be back shortly. I'll be just fine."

Mike made it to the caves and put on his headgear, which had a built-in headlamp. He held a long flashlight in his right hand and an air monitor in his left. About fifty yards into the cave, he saw small eyes on the cave walls and crevices, wide-open eyes, just staring at him.

Then he heard strange, loud sounds, and something flew from the top crevices and right in front of his face. He shined his flashlight on the creature and was so stunned and frightened he almost ran.

Suddenly, the creature spoke: *"You need not fear me, for it is the disobedient that we are here for."*

"Oh heck! You can speak?" Mike, looking startled, yelled.

"You can speak?" the creature asked. *"We've been taught that your kind are ignorant and only good for food!"*

"Food? What are you? Who are you?"

"I am known in the Hebrew language as Abaddon. In the Greek language, I am Apollyon! I am the king of the warring locusts!"

"Warring locusts! What or who are you warring against?"

"Man, obviously! I have been sent to bring judgment on those who do not have the mark of their Maker," Abaddon/Apollyon said.

"Mark? What are you referring to?"

"You don't know? You have the mark, so we can't torment you. We were commissioned by an angel to hurt man during the duration of our season."

"What is your season?"

"It is known to you as five months. For that period, we will torment your kind. I know of you. You're chosen to be the messenger of the world for your kind."

"Messenger? For my kind? What's the message?"

"Tell them that the armies of judgment are here! It's not too late!"

"Not too late for what?"

"You are the messenger! Deliver the message!"

"Not too late for what?" Mike repeated.

Abaddon/Apollyon, still hovering in Mike's face, growled loudly, displaying his canines. Then he angrily flew out of the cave, with millions following him, as he announced, *"We're here! The war has begun!"*

As Mike watched the swarm of locusts exit the cave, he was totally stunned. After he was able to compose himself, he returned to the team. He did not reveal what he'd just experienced; however, the team also saw the swarm of locusts exit the cave.

Mike and his team flew back to Dallas that evening.

CHAPTER
TWENTY-EIGHT

April 4, 2048

L ater that night, Mike called Misty. "Misty, hello."

"Hello, Mike, how did it go out there?"

"Have you ever heard that old saying, 'Some things are better left unsaid'?"

"You found something, yet you don't think you should tell me?"

"I found something, indeed, that I don't think the world is ready for. You know, I heard the story of the Irving, Texas, incident with the runners, and the police portrayed that young man as a nutcase. But what I found out is that he's actually a Christian and a seminary student. Now, I've been called a religious nut myself, as have most committed Christians. What I would like to do is talk to this fellow as well as the others."

"Michael T. Lathan, what did you see? What has you so spooked?"

"It's not just what I saw, but what I experienced! You need to set up a private meeting, if necessary! I can't say anything about it on the phone. I have my dad's reputation to think about. At this meeting, we need Dad, you, me, Rina, Dr. Nealson, Dr. NaHony, Bishop Mark Soloman, Dr. Lucas Timothy, Professor Dodds, and of course, we should try to bring in President Duncan."

"That's a pretty heavy list. Let me see what I can do to coordinate everyone's schedule, and I'll let you know. Sure you don't want to give me a hint?"

"Not without Dad's and Rina's presence so that they can vouch for my sane frame of mind."

"Is it that complex?"

"Complex would be stating it in simple terms. Everyone's going to have to be certain that I'm sane before the meeting starts, because some may have questions about it afterward—even you, my friend."

After hanging up with Mike, Misty touched base with her assistant and staff and gave them an update on her conversation with Mike. Dr. NaHony called the president to set up the confidential meeting.

Monday, April 13, 2048

Everyone who had been invited to join did so, and the meeting was held by holographic telepresence. President Duncan started the meeting.

"Good morning to everyone. I understand that some very important findings will be presented by Dr. Michael T. Lathan Jr. with a message for all. I'm pretty anxious to hear what you have discovered, Dr. Lathan. Dr. Myers, I want to commend you on your continuous hard work. To the Volcano Hazards Program Office Dr. NaHony and Dr. Nealson, you guys have done a phenomenal job in addressing these crises. Also, thank you, Professor Dodds, Professor Rina Adelstein, Rev. Dr. Michael T. Lathan Sr., Bishop Mark Soloman, and Dr. Lucas Timothy for joining us.

"First, I'd like to hear from Dr. Myers and then Michael Jr.—oh,

I'm sorry, our scientist, Dr. Lathan. It must be quite unique for this group to be brought together."

Misty addressed the committee next.

"Good morning, all. It's a pleasure and a privilege to be honored to address this powerhouse group. As you know, more and more strange things have been occurring worldwide. They have been happening with little explanation of how or why. Lately, we've been trying to find out where these giant locusts that have been plaguing the world are originating from. Well, an important, one-word question has surfaced: Why? So, I'm going to let Dr. Michael T. Lathan Jr. have the floor at this time to explain. I would like for him to start with the theory he's been promoting from the beginning. Dr. Lathan, you have the floor."

"Ladies and gentlemen, good morning. I, Dr. Michael T. Lathan Jr., both scientist and Bible scholar, being of sound mind, do swear that what you are about to hear is the whole truth and nothing but the truth. It may inspire some, it might frighten some, it might even offend others, but the fact that it's true will remain. I believe that instead of wasting time over whether it's true or not, we must concentrate heavily on two facts. We've found some insight as to why, coming straight from the horse's mouth. Literally!"

"Literally from the horse's mouth? This is getting very interesting already," President Duncan said.

"Interesting is putting it lightly, sir," Mike said.

"Lightly? Hmm," President Duncan said. "OK, I can't wait. Let's hear what you have."

"First of all, we've all seen what's been happening over the past week now. People are afraid to leave the safety of their own homes. Further, we have seen that not everyone has suffered these attacks. Secondly, these things—these creatures, or whatever you'd like to call them—have been impossible to stop. It's hard enough to see where they're hiding because they just seem to appear from everywhere. Nothing seems to scare them. We've found no way of destroying them. With our weapons systems, Mr. President, we're able to intercept missiles, and we believe we can change the directions of giant meteors. But it's hard to challenge something that is as elusive as these so-called locusts. No chemicals seem to have any effect on them. These things have been observed to wait for people to come outside, only to attack a select few. What we've discovered is that there is a marking on the foreheads of people who are not attacked.

"Yet these things have been seen by the hundreds, hanging around people's jobs, stores, high schools, colleges, and yes, even churches, waiting for the unmarked to step into their buffet line. I say 'buffet' because we all have heard of or have seen people who have been fed on by these things.

"I continue to say 'these things' because though they are called locusts, what I'm about to tell you may, to some, describe something most of us won't know how to classify. Some of you were invited to join us today because of your responses during our clergy meeting and our previous meeting held here, which showed open-mindedness and a willingness to discuss and not refute.

"I was sent to Yellowstone National Park by Dr. Myers, with a team of her choosing. While investigating some hidden caves, I encountered some of these beings—"

A voice interrupted, "OK, OK, Dr. Lathan, you are now calling these things or creatures 'beings'! What exactly are you about to describe—insects, locusts, or some kind of intelligent being?"

"Can we say all of the above?"

Almost everyone responded with questions.

"Please! May we have clarification that would suffice for us all?" President Duncan asked.

"Buckle your seat belt," Mike said. "If you don't have one, just hold on tight. The cave was pitch black, but I could see a few feet in front of me with the lights that I had. About fifty yards into the cave, I heard a strange, loud noise. I noticed the noise was not on the ground but coming from the walls of the cave. As I stared upward, I saw hundreds of what looked like small eyes gazing at me.

"My first reaction was to exit as fast as I could, but my legs wouldn't cooperate. I aimed my flashlight at the wall, and one of the things flew toward me at eye level. I was again startled and momentarily closed my eyes, but out of fear, I opened them to see what it was. Then I saw something I'd only read about."

"Read about, Dr. Lathan? Read about where? Though I may know where you're headed, do you really want to go there?" Dr. Lucas Timothy asked.

"He owes it to us to go there. We've all read about that something, so let us know what you read and saw," Bishop Mark Soloman said.

"What I saw confirms stories I read about that come from Irving, Texas; Naples, Italy; and other places," Mike said. "I saw a face that resembled a man with long hair, the body of a horse, and the tail of a scorpion. It had something around its forehead that resembled a crown, and it had four wings that fluttered faster than those of a hummingbird. It appeared to be dressed for war. Not only that, but it said—"

Several screamed, "It *said*? It said what?"

"Dr. Lathan, do you think that you may have thought you heard it say something? Did any other people report hearing these creatures speak?" President Duncan asked.

"Sir, I don't know what anyone else heard, but I can only confirm what I experienced."

"OK, let's say you did hear something. What in fact do you think you heard?" President Duncan asked.

"It—or he, or whatever—said, 'I am known in the Hebrew language as Abaddon. In the Greek language, I am Apollyon!' He also said that he and his army were sent here by an angel to wage war with humanity who did not have the mark of their Maker. It said that I was to deliver the message. I asked what the message was, and it said, and I quote, 'Tell them that the armies of judgment are here! It is not too late!' Then it said, 'You are the messenger. Deliver the message.' It growled, showed lionlike teeth, and angrily flew out of the cave with what seemed to be millions of others following it."

"There have been no reports of any of these creatures being killed or captured. No chemicals seem to bother them, and we can't find where they're hiding. Why do you think that is?" President Duncan asked.

"The being also said that they had been taught that we're ignorant."

"How ignorant can we be?" President Duncan yelled.

Rev. Dr. Lathan Sr. jumped into the conversation. "With all due respect, Mr. President, we don't seem to be able to kill or capture them. We can't find where they're hiding. How can millions of these beings, or whatever they are, not be found with our technology today?"

"It's quite obvious. Someone doesn't want them found. Why? What could be the real purpose?" Bishop Soloman asked.

"I've done extensive study of and teaching about the book of Revelation," Dr. Timothy said. "If we are to confess belief in the Word of God, the answer to why is before us, if we believe. There's a lot going on in our world that shows total disbelief in that Word. We believe the Word to be true, yet we discard the idea of punishment for the rejection. We hate with our actions toward one another while confessing love and tolerance with our mouths. The answers we seek are not the answers we want. It's been proven since the beginning that total love cannot be achieved at the human level. It can't be forced through catastrophes, pestilence, or wars, yet war is our solution for intolerance. Millenniums bear witnesses to that fact. My opinion is that God is tired of our failure to truly love Him and one another."

"Dr. Michael Lathan Jr. is that your belief?" President Duncan asked.

"Sir, it has been my full theory all along. As a biblical scholar, I have to stand by it. As a scientist, I have to marvel at the fact that science and religion have never been separate. We just force them apart. We try to find a happy medium, but there is none. So, my theory supports the fulfillment of prophecy."

"Say what you are proposing is true," President Duncan said. "What, if anything, can be done concerning these locusts?"

"Their season is to be completed after five months," Bishop Soloman said. "During the rest of that time, I believe the only thing we can do as humans is to change—not just our actions but our hearts as well. You see, Mr. President, if our hearts are purely in the right mode, our actions will reflect it. Human love only has two levels: the love man has for God and the love man has for one another. The first can't be proven except by the presence of the second. These locusts, insects, creatures, or beings are the result of thousands of years of fraudulent love for God."

"But it's just not possible to change the hearts of everyone," President Duncan said.

"That's why the marks on the foreheads are sparingly given," Mike said.

"By whom?" President Duncan asked.

"I think we all know the answer to that one, sir. We must try to convince everyone. Clergy must cross the cultural aisles and work together, or there's no use," Mike said.

"This meeting has been quite different yet informative," President Duncan said. "I'll meet with my advisors, and we'll be getting back to the public later. Thank you, everyone, for such phenomenal research and for the input given today. We have all been enlightened. Dr. Lathan Jr., it has been an eye-opening meeting, to say the least. Truly, you are unique, and I commend you and thank you. You are a brave warrior. Hmm, a talking horse! But Mr. Ed didn't fly! Dr. Myers, thank you for your team and their work in this area. I now put the meeting back into your hands."

Misty then closed the meeting.

* * *

After the meeting, Mike asked Rina to have lunch and said he wanted to discuss something very important with her. As they ate, he suggested that they should put off their wedding until things got back to normal.

Rina, looking very disappointed, said, "I understand, but I was looking forward to us being together very soon."

"We will, I promise. But due to the circumstances, it looks like we are going to be very busy with this locust problem for at least five months. Once this is over, I promise we will get married and be together forever," Mike said.

CHAPTER
TWENTY-NINE

Monday, April 20, 2048

President Duncan called a meeting with the World Health Organization via holographic telepresence. The invitees were representatives from the regional offices, as well as the Global Service Centre.

The meeting was intended to discuss, on an international level, what could be communicated to the public that would promote calm and what plans could be made to protect them from the threat that was plaguing the whole world. They also sought ways to kill these locusts, if it was even possible, and if not, methods to ease the suffering the unmarked people were enduring.

The president also held a separate meeting with military leaders, such as the secretary of defense, the chairman of the Joint Chiefs of Staff, national security advisors, and the secretary of the Department of Homeland Security. In addition, he met with representatives from the US Department of Health and Human Services and the National Oceanic and Atmospheric Administration. The agenda for those meetings included a discussion about the time period for which

Abaddon/Apollyon had told Mike the locusts would remain and to determine if Mike's report was accurate. Each world leader had the responsibility to address their own nation.

Monday, May 4, 2048

President Duncan met with several world leaders by way of holographic telepresence.

"Greetings, everyone. I would like to recognize all of the professional talents and people as well as the representatives of all the nations here. Thank you for joining in to help combine our efforts to soften, if not to alleviate, the suffering around the world.

"First, let me share that we've found it extremely difficult, if not impossible, to rid ourselves of the attacking creatures. Our military has been working tirelessly to find ways to help, but nothing is ridding us of the imminent danger. Our science teams have discovered that they are an extremely intelligent species with the ability to communicate—not only with each other—as they employ strategies of attack and retreat and to keep their base locations unknown. People have been repeatedly preyed upon as a food source. As soon as their wounds heal, they're attacked again.

"Many have become so terrified of the pain and injury that they have attempted suicide, but none have been successful. Some have used firearms, only to be left with wounds and scars that tell of their attempts. There have been several reports of jumpers from buildings, bridges, and even skyscrapers who are left with broken bones, are lame, and are disfigured. There have been hundreds of thousands, if not millions, of cases internationally. I can say that suicide is not the answer.

"One of our decorated science teams and many of our clergy members do believe that there may be prophecy at work. They further believe that our personal and national relationships may be what's driving the attacks. They've said that if people everywhere would improve their attitude toward tolerance on both personal and international levels, these attacks may in fact end.

"I know how preposterous this may sound, but we're running out of possibilities and options. The magnitude of suffering is unimaginable. I can't stand here and tell the world that everyone who is not born again could be a victim, but the evidence is overwhelming and can't be ignored. It may be that a higher power is behind it all. Who's to say that's the only answer. I will say that based on the evidence given, every responsible individual must make a conscious effort to help themselves, seeing that nothing else seems to work. As the world's most powerful man, I will confess that I am a Christian, and neither I nor my family have been attacked. Is that the reason? I can only say that I don't believe that it has hurt us to be born again. So please be diligent in your thoughts, and please make the best decision.

"Those are our findings here. If there have been any successes in any other nations, please share them with the rest of us who are, after several weeks, still under attack. If not, please share what you've heard after this meeting. It could be helpful—maybe the only help. If there's nothing else, I'll answer questions for the next forty-five minutes."

There were so many questions from everyone that the meeting lasted almost another two hours.

* * *

The following day, President Duncan addressed the public.

"Greetings, ladies and gentlemen. As you well know, we have made the announcement of a state of emergency for our nation.

"First, I want to say we've put together several strategic task forces to try to get this situation under control and at the same time keep our citizens safe from being tormented by these stinging and biting locusts, which are attacking people worldwide. We have some very qualified people who have many years of experience in researching and studying how to handle these types of situations.

"Please keep in mind, the world has not had such a devastating and horrific event like this happen during our century. Therefore, we need everyone to please work together as much as possible and adhere to the guidelines that are being put into place. We cannot afford for people to lose control. Therefore, please try to stay calm, and please try your best to stay out of harm's way. These are very trying times for everyone, and I do mean everyone!

"Now I'd like to introduce to you a few of the representatives from the US Department of Health and Human Services, the Centers for Disease Control and Prevention, the Institute for Human Infections and Immunity, the US Department of Education, the Department of Homeland Security, and other related departments.

"Thank you, ladies and gentlemen, for coming forward to take on the responsibility and challenge of making our nation feel as safe as possible and to let people know we are here to help them in any way we can. There will be others working with each department, and you can check online to get their phone numbers. Some departments are short of help due to the situation; therefore, if anyone out there has expertise or any experience in any of these areas, please, please contact that department using the appropriate phone number listed on the screen to see if you can provide assistance.

"I know there is a great amount of fear ramping up in everybody's heart. Even if you're not being attacked, you are still being affected in some way. We have gathered some of the best experts and skilled people who will be heading up these task forces and providing information and instructions to your local city, towns, and rural areas nationwide.

"Please, please, I beg of you, try to be calm and seek the professional guidance and counseling needed in getting us through this. I know many of you have been attacked by these creatures, and several have been hospitalized. Thank God, we have had no fatalities that have been reported here in the nation or abroad. However, there are many people who are in excruciating pain, with a long healing process ahead of them because of the horrific injuries endured by their bodies. I understand the hospitals are overflowing, and many hospitals are seeking volunteers. If you have any medical experience whatsoever or can give a helping hand in any capacity, please contact your local hospital and the Red Cross to let them know you are available, provided you are one of the persons who will not be attacked. However, we do have Kevlar suits and headwear that we can provide for you so that you will have the appropriate gear to combat these monstrous locusts. There is a phone number on the screen for you to contact for protective equipment.

"I don't think we will have to worry about looting or any other crimes, from the reports I'm receiving. There are some who tried, but these creatures attacked them. Maybe that's a good thing, because they could help keep the crime rate down for a while.

"My understanding is there is pertinent information online for each major city, and that website should also be listed on the screen. Please make absolutely sure that you adhere to the guidelines provided on those sites if you want to survive this tragic and catastrophic event.

"We have also been informed that this event will last possibly for five months. That may not seem long to some, but for the people who are being tormented, it may seem like five years or an eternity. Therefore, this may be the longest spring and summer some of you will ever encounter, and I wish to God that it would end right now. I've also been in meetings with some very prestigious and knowledgeable theologians who have informed me that they will be available for people worldwide, 24/7. There will also be churches and other buildings open 24/7 and made available for you to pray and attend church services. They will provide counseling and give you spiritual guidance, if needed.

"There are curfews in place for everyone except those who have been given permission to be out, and they all have badges. Trust me, I don't think you will find too many people trying to get out in these conditions.

"Now, this is hurting our economy drastically in all areas. Therefore, America, brace yourselves for a downfall in the stock market . . . but try to hang in there. We will make a comeback when all this is over. It will take some time to recover, but we will. If you haven't already, please make sure you have first aid kits, nonperishable food items, plenty of consumables, plenty of water, and other life necessities just in case you cannot go out. Please check on your neighbors, senior citizens, and your loved ones. This is the time to be a Good Samaritan. If you've never been one before, here's your opportunity.

"Several prep organizations have been set up to show you how to survive during a major catastrophic event. Those numbers and websites are provided on the screen as well. If you know of anyone who doesn't have any form of communication, please keep them informed of the information that's being broadcast. There is a multitude of information being put together for your use as I speak. Whatever form of broadcast-receiving system you have, please keep it on! Please have something in your home so that you can keep abreast of what's going on.

"Our Department of Education is making preparations for schools to continue education through virtual and online classes for the remainder of the school year. We will keep a watch on this, but the educational system may have to wait until after September to assess what steps must be taken to continue the education process.

"There is so much to be discussed and covered that I can't cover it all now, but as I stated, several task forces have been put in place to assist people everywhere. Please stay connected to some form of local and national news and media outlet, as we will periodically update you of progress in these matters.

"Finally, based on the information I'm receiving about whom

these locusts are attacking, deceivers will wish they had not tried to deceive the locusts by the time the insects are done with them. I'm told there have been people who have attempted to emulate the marks by way of tattoos and face paint, but based on the results, don't try it, because the locusts know the difference.

"Thank you for your time. May God bless you, and may God bless and protect America. Now I ask Rev. Dr. Michael Lathan Sr., if you would, to please lead our nation in a word of prayer."

Every president or leader worldwide held a similar press conference for their region or country.

CHAPTER
THIRTY

Thursday, September 3, 2048

Mike and Rina were having a late lunch at his parents' house. It was a nice summer day as they sat on the swing on the deck in the backyard. They had finally gotten a little rest the night before after being exhausted from a long day's work.

"Today may be the day," Mike said. "Abaddon/Apollyon, the king of the terrible locusts, is supposed to lead the army of locusts from every part of the world back into the bottomless pit from whence they came. It's been five months, give or take a day or two. However, if God is calculating the time frame using our Gregorian calendar, I think I've timed it about right. Everything is supposed to go back to normal."

"I sure hope so. It's been a long, hard, trying five months. So many people are hurting and suffering," Rina said.

"I know. I really feel for them. It's going to take some time for everyone to recover from this. This has been one of the greatest revivals I've seen in my generation, though. So many people have given their lives to Christ and shown love toward one another. Wow!

I've seen so many people reaching out to help others, and the love shown has been breathtaking."

"Let's just hope and pray people don't regress to their hateful and evil ways after the locusts have left and they start to heal. You know how it goes: God sends judgment upon the land, and it seems like all nations, religions, and races come together for one common cause. Yet after many years pass, people go back to their old ways and habits, forgetting about what He brought us out of. I hope it's not so this time. I believe God's really got His message across to the entire world."

"Hopefully, this judgment has brought us all closer to Him and made us know that God is real and that He does get tired of us ignoring His laws and ways. Hmm . . . just when we thought He had gone to sleep, He sent Abaddon/Apollyon to wake us up."

As they were waiting for Mrs. Lathan to let them know when lunch was ready, all of a sudden they heard a very, very loud noise. They looked up and saw Abaddon/Apollyon leading the locusts away, millions of them. They were flying in from the northern, southern, eastern, and western parts of the Earth.

"It's happening! They're leaving!" Mike excitedly called out.

"It is over. Our commission is done here!" Abaddon/Apollyon looked down at Mike and said.

Mike tilted his head to acknowledge Abaddon/Apollyon's voice.

"Mike, he did speak! They're leaving! It's over!" Rina screamed.

They looked at each other in wonder and kissed and hugged, so happy to know that it was over.

Rev. Dr. and Mrs. Lathan ran outside to find out what the excitement was all about and saw the tail end of the locust swarm flying away. They all praised God and started rejoicing, their faces filled with tears.

Afterward, they calmed down and went into the house to sit down and enjoy their lunch. They were talking about everything that had just happened and what had been going on for five long months.

Breaking news flashed across the monitor, with the newscaster announcing that it had been reported from all over the world that the locusts had been seen flying away.

Mike rushed to the monitor and touched the feature that allowed him to see several channels simultaneously. He chose various outlets that featured worldwide news. Each recounted people seeing the locusts leaving their areas in various countries. News reporters who had camped outside with their camera teams just so they would not miss the event, because they had heard that it might happen today, tried to capture the action.

"Wow! This is a great day for us all over the world," a news reporter in Yellowstone National Park said. "I just hope and pray that this horrific event has brought us all closer to loving one another and to realizing that we need each other. We can't blame this on global warming, can we? Back to you, Jack."

Rev. Dr. and Mrs. Lathan and Rina were still at the table, and they all noticed that Mike had a strange look on his face.

"Is there something wrong, Mike?" Rina asked. "You look like you just saw a ghost."

"There are two more woes to come," said Mike, with a sad countenance.

The smiles on the faces at the table faded, and they just sat there staring at one another.

ACKNOWLEDGMENTS

I want to thank my amazing wife, Marilyn. I am continually and eternally grateful for the depth of your commitment to this project and the journey God has laid out for us. Thank you for understanding the importance of my work in the Kingdom of God and for continuously interceding in prayer for me on what I am called by God to do. Thank you so much, sweetheart.

Special thanks to Marinna Castilleja, Kirkus Senior Production Editor for *WOE 1: 2038–2048*, along with the entire Kirkus Book Prep team, all of whom put in so much time, effort, and dedication to ensure this novel was professionally edited, formatted, and book cover designed.

Thank you also to the book cover illustrator, Patigonart, for your impressive artwork, which made my book cover vision come to life.

Special thanks to Jason McCoy, Jeremy McCoy, and the entire team on this *WOE 1: 2038–2048* book project. Thank you for your commitment, trusting and believing in the gift that God has given me to minister through writing. I am so blessed to have each of you as such a powerful support team and I thank you all for volunteering your assistance.

ABOUT THE AUTHOR

Nathan Scott is an ordained minister and published author. He has worked in the aviation industry for over twenty-five years and in 2002 was awarded a utility patent from the United States Patent and Trademark Office for an Improved Door Security Striker Fastening Plate and Method. He currently lives in Texas with his wife, Marilyn.

9 789898 568 7002